AF269076

Zinnia ♥

CHRIS KENISTON

Indie House Publishing

Indie House Publishing

BOOKS BY CHRIS KENISTON

Hart Land
Heather
Lily
Violet
Iris
Hyacinth
Rose
Calytrix
Zinnia

Farraday Country
Adam
Brooks
Connor
Declan
Ethan
Finn
Grace
Hannah
Ian
Jamison
Keeping Eileen
Loving Chloe

Aloha Series Heartwarming Edition
Aloha Texas
Almost Paradise
Mai Tai Marriage
Dive Into You
Look of Love

Love by Design
Love Walks In
Flirting with Paradise

Surf's Up Flirts
(Aloha Series Companions)
Shall We Dance
Love on Tap
Head Over Heels
Perfect Match
Just One Kiss
It Had to Be You

**Other Books
By Chris Keniston**

Honeymoon Series
Honeymoon for One
Honeymoon for Three

Family Secrets Novels
Champagne Sisterhood
The Homecoming
Hope's Corner

Original Aloha Series
Waikiki Wedding

ACKNOWLEDGEMENTS

I have a few extra people to tip my hat to this time around. As usual without my author friends Kathy Ivan, Barb Han, and Linda Steinberg, *Zinnia* would still be floundering mid-story. For inspiring my muse, I have my sister-in-law Sheri Keniston to thank for sharing all her knowledge of executive assistants to the movers and shakers, and my childhood friend Lisa Alves Drace for enlightening me the ways of the world.

A shout out to my friend Linda Borgia for her eagle eye in proofing, and to the late Sid Borgia, father of my friend and fan James Borgia, and famed NBA referee who gave us the expression "no harm, no foul."

I hope y'all enjoy reading *Zinnia* and the latest happenings at Hart Land!

CHAPTER ONE

"So help me if that phone rings one more time, I'm throwing it out the window." Zinnia Colby glanced at the business line's caller ID and sighed. "Grams, I'd better call you back."

"Very well, dear, maybe I'll know more of the upcoming schedules by the time I hear from you." As her grandmother cut off the call, Zinnia wished she could be at the lake helping prep for her cousin Heather's wedding instead of at her desk fielding phone calls and juggling schedules. From organizing political dinners to buying and moving prized artwork, she loved the excitement and diversity of her new career—most days. Today was not one of them. Today she wanted to be at the lake dodging Lucy's matchmaking efforts and oohing and aahing over some ill-fated craft effort of Grams, and most of all, enjoying the cousins she loved as much as her own sister, Iris.

Reaching for the landline, she did her best to plaster on a smile that no one would see, and hoped that she could project some sense of Zen to her over-eager caller. "Hello?"

"It's not here," a frantic male voice blurted out.

"Did you not get the tracking link I sent you?"

"Yes. It's supposed to be here today."

Quickly, Zinnia followed the link she'd sent her boss Sam's public relations guru. "It's out for delivery."

"The mailman already came by."

She pinched the bridge of her nose and breathing deeply, let her cousin Violet's ever calm voice encouraging tranquility play in the back of her mind. Zinnia's lungs might be full of New York City oxygen, but her Zen was nowhere to be found. "It's not coming regular mail. Silvianna's assistant assured me courier service was the best way for the garment to be there by tomorrow's shoot."

In order to arrange for this photo shoot of her boss, a respected businessman and philanthropist from one of Connecticut's oldest families, spending a casual weekend at the Hamptons home of a retired and well-loved politician, while hanging about in the never-before-seen outfit from the hottest new designer for the movers and shakers of the country, by the current popular photographer de jour, Zinnia had promised and horse traded with no fewer than half a dozen people. All it would take for the whole plan to fall to pieces was for one link in the chain to break loose. As it was, they only had two hours to pull it all off since both her boss and his host had other pressing appointments. Crafting the illusion of a new and upcoming rat pack with two respected powerhouses, hanging out by the relaxing seashore took a hell of a lot of time and coordination. And it was that last quality for which Zinnia had her grandfather to thank. No one maneuvered complex situations like the United States Marine Corps.

"Just remember, you promised a Silvianna exclusive," Sam had stated, as if there was any chance she would have forgotten.

Nor would she forget all the other promises that had to be made to procure the right house from the right power broker and the right designer. And who knew it mattered where the chocolate-dipped fruit came from or that the quinoa balls and shrimp bruschetta on the Tiffany—had to be Tiffany—silver platter, that no one was going to have time to taste anyhow, would have to be gluten free. "Everything will be fine." And if she repeated that enough times, she might believe it herself.

Barefoot, with faded jeans, no shirt, and dark wavy hair spiked out in every direction, her boss padded into the room. "Morning."

"Morning," she muttered back at him before returning to the PR guy's call. "I'll follow up on that delivery and let you know if there's any delay. Otherwise, we'll see everyone on Saturday."

"PR?" Sam asked.

Zinnia nodded. "You'd think the man had never coordinated a lead article for a major popular magazine in his life."

"That's probably why he's been at the top of his business for so long."

"Maybe." She wasn't convinced. This was her first time orchestrating the back end of a major branding effort and no one saw her falling apart at the seams.

Collapsing onto the sofa as if he hadn't just rolled out of bed at three o'clock in the afternoon, Sam took a long swig from the mug in his hand. "I'm heading home tonight."

That was not what Zinnia wanted to hear. "We have the shoot the day after tomorrow. It's a long drive from here. I thought you were going home after that?"

He drained the last of his coffee and shook his head. "Something's come up."

"Something?" It wasn't like him to be so vague. Not with her. Nor was it like him to take off after having worked so hard to build his position in the community.

"Nothing serious. At least I hope not. A few things to straighten out for my mom."

"I hope everything works out for your mother. She's a nice lady." The whole family was pretty nice considering they were dripping with money. Besides his three vacation homes in the Caribbean, the south of France and the west coast, he kept this penthouse apartment overlooking Central Park, and a suburban home in Connecticut. The latter two worlds as different as night and day. She'd only had the privilege of viewing the Connecticut cottage—all six thousand square feet of it—before Sam and his family had moved in. Tasked with what she did best, liaise between Sam and whoever had been contracted for whatever job, she'd coordinated with the interior decorator and done a last minute walk through and punch list just before Sam had unpacked his bags. To this day he had no idea the master bedroom had ever been painted the wrong color, the beam for the open concept had been replaced—twice—or that if the designer had had her way, there'd have been a nine foot wall of mirrors in the bedroom.

"I'll be back here Friday night. Plenty of time to get to the Hamptons on Saturday." Tipping his head in her direction, he winked. "Couldn't let my best girl down."

There was no point in rolling her eyes at him. The charm oozed from him as organically as *sir* or *ma'am* slid from the lips of an enlisted man. Besides, she'd grown used to his attitude over time and understood there was no disrespect intended. She blamed the attitude on the apartment. The trappings of a flashy New York penthouse without the signs of a loving family in the burbs brought out the carefree teen hidden in every middle-aged man.

"I've decided," he sat up, resting his arms on his knees, "that after the shoot, I'm taking time off until the meeting in Albany."

Zinnia felt her brows press high on her forehead. "That's almost four weeks." What was the point of all the push if he was going to pull back?

The lazy grin he was so famous for when doing live interviews took over his face. "I know."

"You want me to cancel everything on the schedule?"

He shook his head. "I'll do the audio interviews, but nothing that involves driving into Manhattan. I've already told the rest of my team I'm out for the duration."

"Okay." The rest of the team being his campaign manager, strategist, publicist, and most likely hair stylist and driver. For Zinnia, this was a first. From day one after she'd been hired on as his personal project manager, a glorified title for general all-around keeper and coffeemaker, she'd been running at full speed practically twenty-four seven, forcing her to step back from her other high-profile clients. What the heck was going on?

"Since I won't be setting foot here or at the office, you can work from wherever you want."

"Wherever?" Her voice rose to match the raising of her brows again.

Sam chuckled. "Yes. Wherever. Even your country lake."

"Now you're talking!" It took her a split second to grab her phone and tap out the familiar number.

"Hello, dear."

"Good news, Grams. Have Lucy clean up Mom's cottage."

"About that—"

She rambled on without waiting for her grandmother's thought. "I'm coming to the lake on Sunday and staying till the wedding!"

"That's almost four weeks."

"Yes, ma'am."

For the next few minutes all she could hear was Lucy squealing along with what sounded like Poppy or maybe Lily in the background. Already the sound of home lifted her spirits. Life didn't get any better than this.

●　●　●　●

"If I never get another group text on faculty meetings in my lifetime, it will be too soon."

"One of those days?" David Ingram's grandfather chuckled into the phone. "There's a reason law school professors, or any educator for that matter, get summers off. It's the only way to prevent the entire faculty from being arrested for murdering their department heads."

"I believe it."

"Next time I get the bright idea to help the dean out by teaching summer school, feel free to lock me in a closet somewhere until I come to my senses."

That last line had his grandfather laughing literally out loud. "At least you have a choice. I pretty much had to do whatever Uncle Sam wanted."

And Uncle Sam's travel agent wasn't always the kindest. The thought doused David's complaints. There were worse things in life than dealing with overwhelmed first year law students who, like their teacher, would rather be anywhere else than locked in four concrete walls all day long. "I don't know how you did it."

"It was easy. I loved it. Most of the time."

That's the answer his grandfather always gave. He had a handful of old cronies from his West Point days who had either kept in touch, or had reconnected recently at a reunion. To hear his grandfather talk about his friends and their careers, anyone would think their lives had been one big frat party instead of the hell it often was.

"When does the semester end?"

"Thank heaven, this is finals week. But I'm still going to have to sequester myself long enough to get a promised article for the University Law Journal on paper."

"You could write those with your eyes closed and you know it."

"Usually I'd agree with you, but this one is worse than pulling stubborn teeth."

"What you need is sun and fresh air."

"What I need is a muse."

"Okay, sun, fresh air and a muse," his grandfather deadpanned. "And I know just the place."

"Oh, I don't like the sound of that."

"How can you not like it when I haven't said anything?"

"I recognize the tone. It was the same one that said I would enjoy a summer at teenage boot camp."

"Kamp Kiwi?"

"I've vanquished that name from my vocabulary."

"You're crazy. That's a great summer camp for boys."

"You mean for little Marines."

His grandfather harrumphed.

"I'm not kidding, Gramps. I know full grown Marines who would have cried at the morning calisthenics. Ten year olds are not supposed to be able to do chin ups."

"You were eleven."

"Barely." David couldn't believe he was laughing at the memory. At the time he thought it was hell. Up before the dawn, making their own bunks until you could bounce a quarter on the sheets, and a morning obstacle course—all before breakfast. The mere thought of it still made him cringe. Though he would never admit to the old man that he loved the archery, the victory tower, and crew. Just not enough to grow up and follow his grandfather's career in the military.

"Doesn't change that you need a little R&R and I happen to know just the right place."

He really wouldn't mind getting out of Dodge for a bit, and

reservations on short notice never bode well. "How right?"

"Harold, General Hart, has cottages for rent by a beautiful, tranquil lake. I happen to know they have empty cabins. I was thinking of dropping anchor for a few weeks but your grandmother wants to go visit her sister instead."

"General?"

"Don't make it sound like I said Attila the Hun. He's retired and taking life easy."

Somehow the words *general* and *easy* seemed to go together about as well as oil and water. "I don't know."

"There's nothing to lose. If you don't like the peace and quiet then you can always leave and write your paper in that stuffy apartment you call home."

"It's not stuffy." It wasn't his fault that his Manhattan apartment building had been around since before the Brooklyn Bridge. Still, his grandfather's suggestion did hold some appeal. He hadn't been in the mountains since college.

"Harold's granddaughter owns *the* Pastry Stop."

"The bakery?" Open less than a year, the Pastry Stop had managed to build a reputation that stretched from the small mountain town all the way to big city Boston and had made its way onto the popular must try eateries lists for the northeast.

"The one and only."

His grandfather was right. What did he stand to lose? "Empty cabin?"

"Yours for the taking."

"Okay. Thank you." An easy rap on the door reminded him that he was still working and not quite ready for a mountain escape. "I have to go, Gramps. Talk to you before next week. Give my love to Gramma."

"Will do."

He disconnected the call and turned to the door. "Come in."

"Professor Ingram?" A slender young man in need of a haircut inched his way into the small office.

"How can I help you?"

The kid shoved his glasses higher on the bridge of his nose and momentarily pressed his lips between his teeth.

Anyone would think that the kid was facing Genghis Khan and not a mere law professor. Regardless of his credentials.

"I was wondering if there was any way I could take the final, uh, early?"

"Early?" That was a new one on him. Most kids would prefer to put off an exam for as long as possible. David scrambled through his memory banks of the two classes he was teaching, but with a couple of hundred kids per lecture hall, there was no way he could pinpoint which class this young man was in. "You're in…"

"Constitutional law." The kid straightened and looked almost proud. There was clearly a story here. "I'm Jason Baker."

"Have a seat, Jason." No sense in making the poor guy stand at attention like a new recruit shaking in his boots. Turning to his computer, David hit a few keys and pulled up Jason's record. He was in both of the classes David taught and doing quite well. It took a few more strokes to see the kid's academic history. No red flags of any kind. "Tell me why you want to take the test early."

"I have a …personal conflict on the scheduled date. And I'd rather get it over with sooner than try and push it off until after… well, after."

One of the perks of practicing and teaching law for as long as he had was that he'd become very good at recognizing a stellar performance. This kid was as sincere as they came, and troubled. "Maybe you should fill me in on some of the details?"

Jason swallowed slow and hard. For a moment, David thought the kid might be fighting tears. "Since my dad died when I was in high school, it's been just my mom and my two little sisters."

"I'm sorry for your loss." The words always seemed so empty but silence was worse.

The kid nodded. "Anyhow, Mom's going to need surgery. Right away."

That never sounded good.

"The doctors scheduled it for the same day as the Constitutional law final. If it were just me I could take it since I'd only be in the hospital waiting anyhow, but my youngest sister is pretty scared."

"And you want to be with your sister?"

Jason nodded.

He certainly couldn't fault his student for that. As a matter of fact, for someone as young as Jason, having so much concern for his little sister was quite admirable. "I'm sure we can work something out."

Relief washed over the young man's face and David had to fight not to pull him into a hug and let him know everything was going to be just fine. Twenty-two might be the age of legal adulthood, but it was awfully young to be responsible for two younger sisters and an infirmed mother.

"Thank you." Jason ran his hands along the sides of his jeans.

David had worked with enough students to interpret some of their body language outside the classroom. This kid was itching for someone to talk to. "How is your mom?"

"Strong. She's strong."

It sounded like Jason was trying to convince himself more than anyone else. "If it's not too intrusive, what is she going in for?"

"Uterine cancer."

No wonder they were all worried. Cancer was a terrifying word for most people. Especially when the word mother came on its heels. "I'm sure the doctor has explained the positive survival rate with most uterine cancers?"

He nodded. "Averages eighty percent."

"Most are better." His family history with cancer had given him hours of fact finding he'd never forgotten.

Jason nodded again, but didn't make an effort to move or speak.

How had David missed the pain in the kid's eyes? The question was where to start, how to ease the fear. Heaving a sigh, it was time to break the cardinal rule and get personal. "When I was in college my mother was diagnosed with breast cancer. By the time she'd gone to the doctor it had spread to her lymph nodes."

The way Jason's eyes rounded wide, David knew he understood the gravity of the situation.

"If you're any good at math, no need to mention that was a very long time ago. The doctors weren't as optimistic as we'd have liked." Jason blinked quickly and David hurried on. "Dad took her to Hawaii last month for her birthday."

The light of hope sparked in Jason's eyes.

"Your mom has way better odds. And with kids who care about her as much as you obviously do, she has plenty of motivation to do as the doctors tell her."

"That's what the doctor said, but," his gaze lifted to the nearby window, "it's nice to hear from someone else. Someone who knows how it feels."

David pulled out a card from his desk, turned it over and scribbled his cell phone number on the back before extending it to the student. "Take this. It has my cell phone number on the back. Feel free to call me any time you want to talk. Day or night."

Jason nodded.

"I want you to promise me." He remembered all too well how scared he'd been of losing his mom, and he'd still had a dad and grandparents to reassure him.

"Yes, sir."

"I mean it."

"Thank you."

A few more words, and a scheduled test time, and David watched the young man walk out the door and down the hall. Never had he been so thankful for whoever invented cell phones. Now if only the kid would use it.

CHAPTER TWO

"Of all the months for Mom to channel Aunt Becky's redecorating gene." Zinnia stood in the doorway of her mother's summer cabin and stared at the gaping two by fours. What had once been a cozy cabin was now nothing more than a shell with free standing supports in a few key places to stop the ceiling from crashing down on them.

Heather Preston, her eldest cousin and the bride to be, hefted her shoulders in a pained apology. "If it makes you feel any better, not to be outdone, Mom has torn up all the bedrooms again so we'll both be staying at Hart House while I'm here. And I'm here a lot more than usual for the next few weeks."

"Well," Zinnia blew out a tired sigh and sprouted a slow smile, "*that* is definitely a perk."

Linking elbows with her cousin, Heather leaned into Zinnia. "Now, tell me all about this new career of yours."

"Not much to tell." Just eager enough not to want to jinx her newfound opportunity all those months ago, Zinnia had kept her mouth shut. Stalling informing her family about the shift in her work since she was first approached by Sam after one of his friends and her clients had raved about her level of efficiency. Then she'd learned about the exclusivity clause and the non-disclosure agreements she'd be signing. Quickly, once her own lawyer looked things over, she discovered the thing was so airtight there wasn't a whole lot she could tell even if she wanted to. Which worked fine when she was in New York City and all of her family were scattered about New England, but there was no way she would survive almost four weeks at the lake without sharing *something*. "I'm doing admin work."

Heather stopped walking and spine snapped straight, narrowed her laser-like gaze at Zinnia. "All this secrecy over admin. Really?"

"Really."

Heather relaxed her stance, but not the intensity of her stare.

"Admin can cover quite a bit of territory. Can we get a little more specific?"

"You know, handling the details of day to day business." A lot of business. It had taken her more days than she'd expected to clear her boss's schedule and reorganize everything in preparation for a few weeks on the lake.

"Details?"

Zinnia shook her head. She probably should have thought her answers through better before showing up at Hart Land. It would have been easier to deal with the Spanish Inquisition.

Arms crossed, Heather all but tapped her toes. "Why so secretive?"

"I'm not being secretive." *Not exactly*. She took a step forward. "There's just not much to tell. You know. Same old same old, day in and day out."

"That's what the Genoveses said." Heather shortened her steps.

Zinnia cocked her head to one side at her cousin. "The drugstore?"

Shaking her head, Heather rolled her eyes. "The crime family. You know. Mafia."

"Oh, for heaven's sake." She threw her hands up. "You sound more like a suspense writer than a doctor. Maybe you're channeling Cindy's husband."

"Obviously, I'm teasing. I know you wouldn't work for the mob." Heather stopped short again and narrowed her gaze at Zinnia before shaking her head. "But it's not like you to be so reserved. Do you like the job?"

"Oh, yes."

"Well, that's good to hear. We were all pretty concerned when you just up and left your last job after only being there a short while."

What her cousin wasn't saying was that Zinnia's boredom factor was so high, she had a challenge staying put. Never left one job till she had another, she wasn't irresponsible, but just bored too easily. "So far it's kept me on my toes, that's for sure. And it's diverse enough to keep me from losing interest."

"Sounds good so far."

"It is. Though there's nothing exciting about having to make reservations for my boss's travel, but it's fun when I get to go shopping and spend someone else's money."

"Okay, shopping with someone else's money does not sound much like admin."

"Oh, trust me. I'm up to my ears in files and data, but I'm on minimum workload for the next few weeks." She took the porch steps at a quick clip, then spun around before shoving the front door open and practically squealed at her cousin. "Because we've a wedding countdown!"

A huge grin spread across Heather's face. "That we do."

"There you are." Arms open wide and dressed in a floor length royal blue kaftan with gold embroidery edgework, her grandmother looked like a human masterpiece. "We were expecting you hours ago."

"I ran into construction leaving the city."

"And I ran into her when she pulled in. We took a detour to see what Aunt Marissa is doing to the cottage."

Grams sighed through a smile. "Sometimes I think my girls should have started a construction company all their own."

"Ha. I can just see Mom now, wielding a hammer." Heather smiled at her grandmother.

"Oh." Her grandmother's expression turned serious. "I almost forgot. Dr. Harris called for you. Said your phone was going straight to voice mail."

"I'd better see what that's all about. I'm supposed to be off rotation till after the honeymoon." At a quick clip, Heather took off for the landline in the kitchen.

"I hope it's nothing serious." Zinnia looked across the large foyer.

"Me too, dear. This break between her job in Boston and opening the new hospital is the first long vacation she's had since she was in high school." Resting one hand on the newel post of the grand staircase, Grams straightened her shoulder and smiled up at her. "Let's get you settled in and then we can discuss the wedding over tea and warm cookies."

"What kind of cookies?" Zinnia had already made peace with needing a larger dress size after eating at the lake for a few weeks.

"Sptizbuben."

Her stomach rumbled and she made an executive decision. "Settling in can wait. Let's see if Lucy needs some help in the kitchen."

"Help. *Right*." Grams smiled and led the way.

Who was Zinnia trying to fool? She'd never been able to resist anything warm and sweet that came out of the Hart Land kitchen.

Swerving away from the oven door, Lucy set a warm tray of cookies on a cooling rack and glanced up. "Well, look who finally made it home." If not for the twinkling blue eyes and soft grin, the stern words would have been taken more seriously.

"Nice to see you too, Lucy."

At that moment, Heather hung up the phone.

"Anything serious?" Grams asked.

Lucy's smile slipped, her words tumbling over Gram's question. "Are you going to have to go back?"

"No. Just a little last minute business."

"Oh, I wish you hadn't used that word." Zinnia heaved a deep sigh.

"Business?" Grams asked.

Zinnia nodded. "I have to send a quick email that I almost forgot about." She grabbed a cookie with her fingertips and let it fall back onto the tray.

"They have to cool," Lucy admonished.

Her grandmother took a seat. "You may have a little trouble with the internet."

"I know. I'll use the wired computer in the General's office."

Grams shook her head. "Won't be much help. Our internet is down."

That was not what she needed to hear. She didn't have much work to do, but what little she had was important and it would take a lot longer if she was going to have to hunt around the property for a workable connection. At least she had one thing to look forward to on her hunt—peace and quiet and one heck of a workplace view.

• • • •

So far, so good. David had left for the lake first thing in the morning at the break of dawn. By lunchtime, he was driving down Main Street. The picturesque storefronts, including the barber pole outside of Floyd's, the towering trees and winding roads, combined to make the small town everything his grandfather had led him to expect.

Nothing was disappointing. A warm and friendly greeting from the Irish lady at the quaint general store, the One Stop, had gone above and beyond his expectations. Even now, thinking about how the woman who had introduced herself as Katie had packed him up with enough groceries and suitable snacks for the duration as if she'd been his mother instead of a newly introduced shopkeeper, made him want to smile.

But the final etching on the perfect place to unwind from a long school year stood proud and strong in front of him as he turned off the main road. Hart House. "Not bad, Gramps."

Pulling into an open space at the foot of the circle drive, he slipped out of the front seat and admired the treetops kissing the deep blue backdrop. The sky had to be this bright in New York. After all, it was the same sky. Still, had it really been this blue when he'd turned off the Hutch onto Interstate 95?

"Welcome."

David snapped around at the greeting.

"The forecast is pretty much the same for the rest of the week."

"Good to know." He moved toward the woman with chin length silver hair and a smile that made her blue eyes sparkle.

"I'm Fiona Hart. The General has been looking forward to meeting you."

"I look forward to meeting him as well."

"I hope you haven't made supper plans yet?" The woman took the steps to the porch with the mobility of a much younger woman. "The General is expecting you to join us. Lucy, our housekeeper, has made her lasagna."

"My favorite." He'd picked a good day to arrive.

"Yes." Fiona Hart paused at the top of the steps and David hurried around her to hold the front door open. "Your grandfather told us." That shouldn't have come as a surprise. After all, his grandfather was a longtime friend of the General.

The aroma of home cooked gravy simmering smacked him as he followed her into the spacious front hall. Bless his grandfather. David wasn't starving himself, but he hadn't been enjoying home cooked meals either.

"Follow me and I'll give you the key. Your cabin is just down the hill. The one with the yellow door. Lovely view of the water."

"Thank you."

Stopping at a huge antique desk, she rummaged in a drawer and withdrew a traditional key with a large yellow pom pom attached. "Have you had lunch? Lucy made chicken salad this afternoon."

"Again, thank you, but I have some work to do and groceries in the car."

"Oh, did you meet Katie?" The bright smile lit her face again.

"I did." He was sure his smile matched his hostess's.

"Then I'm sure you're well stocked."

"Yes, ma'am." Slipping the key into his pocket, he waited for more paperwork. When he realized there was none coming, he took a step back and remembered the final grades he needed to complete and upload. With any luck, he'd have them done before dinner tonight. "Is there a password for the internet?"

"I'm afraid not."

"No password?" An open internet for guests was going to prove to be a problem for him.

"Well, no."

"Oh, good. Then it is a secured line?"

"Well, no." She closed the drawer and looked up at him. Her amused grin told him she was reading his confusion loud and clear. "There is no internet in the cabins."

"No internet?" Confusion had no doubt blossomed into total shock. Everyone had internet nowadays. It was downright barbaric not to have some sort of Wifi service.

Fiona Hart nodded, her grin intact. "The whole purpose of the lake is to unplug and enjoy the world around you."

He had no problem with enjoying the world around him, but the unplugging thing was all together different. "How do you operate without internet? Take reservations?"

"Oh, we have wired internet here at Hart House. The General has learned to take advantage of online communication with old friends."

The ripple of panic that was beginning to take root deep in his gut quickly ebbed. "Do you think the General would have a problem if I worked a little from the house here? I have final reports to upload."

"I'm sure he wouldn't mind at all."

"Good."

"If the internet worked."

"If?"

Fiona Hart nodded. Her pleasant disposition intact. "It stopped working a few days ago. We're waiting on the technician."

"I see. What time is he coming?"

"Between noon and four pm."

Oh good. He could get online and ship off his data before nightfall.

"Monday," Fiona Hart finished.

Maybe coming here hadn't been such a good idea after all.

"Some of the guests use the internet with their top hots."

"Top hots?" Top hots made no… realization dawned. "Hot spot."

Fiona smiled up at him. "If you say so. They work best away from the trees. Or above them."

Above them? David shook his head slowly. Not such a good idea at all.

• • • •

I love the lake. I love the lake. Zinnia shifted the lounge chair a foot closer to the Point. She'd been out here for an hour. Or maybe closer to two. Her morning had started out just fine. With only a few minutes of work to do, she should have been done and at the main house hanging out with her cousins. Working on the wedding plans. There was always something to be decided for a wedding that would include half the town on its guest list, and she wanted to be included. Except first she needed to get this paperwork emailed to her boss's manager sooner than later. And with every rolling wave of the easy tide, later seemed more likely.

Once again, as she'd done at least a hundred times so far, she double checked that her cell phone hot spot was still on, then checked her computer was connected to the hot spot, and then disconnected her laptop's connection and reconnected in hopes that this time the information would go through.

No joy. She stood and took a step toward the shore, praying for all the pretty connection bars. "This is crazy," she muttered to herself. Elevating the laptop with one hand, she focused on the little row of bars, or lack of rows.

"Blast." Dropping like a led laced pretzel, she sank to the sandy ground, bent over, and slid a striped towel over her head to better see the screen. Like a miracle from above, the bars appeared bright and green. Now things were cooking with gas. A slew of emails appeared in her inbox. "Double blast." She'd have to go through all of them to make sure nothing had to be handled yesterday. On the sand, hunched over, the towel draped above like a saggy canopy, she typed away, not daring to move even one inch in case the nice dark bars changed their mind and disappeared. She was almost afraid to breathe. Just one more copy and paste and she could return to the house and suck in a warm, fresh… "Oomph."

Zinnia inhaled a hard breath. Her thin laptop flew from her hands and an elephant slammed into her—hard—knocking her forward. She felt her knee stretch seconds before her legs unfolded beneath her and she face planted in the grainy sand, the elephant and his laptop landing beside her.

Only the elephant might tackle like an NFL linebacker, but it didn't look a darn thing like an elephant. Arm stretched out beside him, a tall, fair skinned human being—male human being—laid silently on his back. It took her rattled brain cells a few seconds to assess the situation.

Eyes squeezed shut, the definitely male specimen groaned and flung a heavy arm across her midsection. Immediately she updated her assessment. Most definitely male and most definitely a *fine* specimen.

CHAPTER THREE

Opening one eye, David looked straight up to the blue sky and wondered how the heck had he gone from searching for a decent hot spot connection to sprawled on his back on the sand. "What happened?"

"I was just going to ask you the same thing."

Turning in the direction the soft voice had come from, he realized that not only was he prostrate on the sand, he was dangerously close to being atop the person connected to the soothing voice. Where had she come from? Firing slower than usual, his brain finally managed to convey to his arm that it was time to move. It was one thing to accidentally land on a member of the opposite sex, it was another to remain in such close contact indefinitely. Easing his hand away and bringing it to rest across himself, he ignored the discomfort radiating from his shoulder to his fingertips. "I was searching for a decent hot spot connection."

"Did you find it?" A hint of humor seemed to embrace her words.

He gave a curt nod, immediately recognizing his mistake. The headache coming on was going to be a doozy. "Sort of. It appears my hot spot reception only starts at five feet above the ground."

"Or under a foot."

Unless a man knew a woman in the biblical sense, flat on his back was no way to carry on a conversation with this lady. Especially one with such a captivating voice and a profile to match. Pushing off on his good elbow, he brought himself to an upright position, thankful he didn't see stars. "I'm pretty sure I have no idea what you're talking about, and beginning to doubt if I have any idea what I'm talking about."

As the blonde untangled herself from a colorful towel and sat up, he could see her face was as pretty as her profile. "The only place I've been able to get a decent enough reception to upload some files was down here at shore level."

"Under a foot from the ground," he repeated her earlier words. "Which would explain why I didn't notice you until it was too late. Sorry about that." Not that he would have noticed her even if she'd been sitting up in a regular chair. So focused on the bars at the bottom of his screen, David hadn't exactly been watching where he was walking. He'd been sidestepping, holding his laptop up high and keeping the screen away from the sun. *Laptop.* What had he done with his laptop?

Moving his other arm, his fingertips knocked against something cold and hard. Glancing over to his left, there was the laptop, lid open, perched awkwardly in the sand. From where he sat he could see the screen was intact, but he didn't want to think what all that sand, if it got in his computer, would do to his data. And without Internet, who knew how he was going to access back up. Of course if there was sand in his computer it wouldn't matter if he could access back up. The sleek hunk of metal would be virtually useless to him.

Suddenly it dawned on him, maybe he'd hit his head even harder than he'd thought. He'd just spent the last five minutes sitting next to—okay, maybe most of that had been spent sprawled out beside—a beautiful young woman, and he had not had the wherewithal to ask her name or apologize properly or make sure she wasn't injured. "Are you okay?"

A slight smile touched her lips. "Define okay."

He bit back a grin. He deserved that. "Let's start with any broken bones? Internal injuries? Should I be calling 911?"

"No. No. And no. So I guess," she raised her hands and wiggled her fingers then did the same with her toes, "I'm doing all right."

"That's good. I am sorry." The wave of relief caught him off guard.

The blonde with the kind smile stuck her hand out. "Zinnia Colby."

"David Ingram." He probably held onto her hand a moment longer than he should have, but something about her felt so… familiar. Or maybe comfortable was a better word. Or maybe he was just overtired from a crazy long school year and one too many courtroom appearances. His attention drifted over to the laptop a few inches ahead of them. "We should probably check for damages."

Zinnia—he liked that name—nodded and extended her arms forward, her entire body stretching like a lazy cat woken from a nap. Her fingers wrapping around the portable computer, she drew it onto her lap. For a second he almost thought she might be praying over it, before she lifted the lid and tapped at the keys.

"Here goes." Her gaze remained intent on the screen when the corners of her lips slowly tipped north and a broad smile took over her face. "No damage here. How about you?"

Holding his breath and saying a silent prayer, he did the same with his laptop as she'd done, without the lithe stretch. Lid open, he blew the few grains of sand away that had managed to make themselves at home on his keyboard and gave a mental fist pump when the screen came to life. "No harm, no foul." He noticed her rubbing her knee and frowned. "Are you sure you're all right?"

"Fine." At full wattage, her smile was even more powerful.

"Then why," he pointed to her leg, "are you rubbing your knee?"

Immediately her gaze dropped to her leg and she seemed surprised to discover all was not fine. "Must have tweaked it a bit when I fell over."

"Again, my apologies. When I glanced this way from my door, I hadn't noticed anyone."

"Which door?"

"The yellow one."

"Oh. Then you're the friend's grandson?"

"If the friend is Commander Ingram, then yes. You know my grandfather?"

"Afraid not. Had never heard of him until Lucy mentioned we were expecting a new guest. I should, in all fairness, warn you. Lucy is a bit of a misdirected yenta."

"Excuse me?"

"She thinks she's a real life Dolly Levy, matchmaker extraordinaire. Bound and determined to find people the love of their lives, never mind that she has a track record to prove otherwise. And you, Mr. Ingram, are fresh meat."

• • • •

The way his eyes popped open anyone would think Zinnia had announced he'd be sacrificed at dawn to appease the volcano Gods. Though, in some ways that wasn't too far off from the truth.

"Excuse me?"

"You said that already." She probably shouldn't tease the poor guy. It was bad enough she'd just sent him flying a few minutes ago because she too wasn't expecting anyone else on the beach at this hour. At least not without warning from someone most likely squealing for joy and accompanied by an equally noisy family, all congregating loudly, ready for a vacation of fun in the sun. "According to conversation at the dinner table last night, the only thing the General seemed sure of is that none of his friend's grandchildren are married. Which means you must be single."

He nodded, but that startled look in his eyes hadn't completely disappeared.

"And if you checked in alone…." She waited for some confirmation.

It took a moment before he verified her supposition. "I did."

She smiled. "Then Lucy is bound to find someone she believes perfect for you. Or more likely, imperfect."

"I'm not looking for someone, perfect or otherwise."

"Oh," she waved his words away, "that has little to do with it."

Recognition must have dawned because the startled look disappeared with a blink, and a nod of understanding took its place. "Hence, the warning that I have excellent potential to be an unwilling patsy?"

"That about covers it."

"Thank you for the advisement, but you can rest assured that my only plan for my stay is to get some work done, *alone*, and enjoy a little fresh mountain air while I'm at it. There is no room for matchmaking anywhere in the schedule."

"Aunt Zinnia!" And unlike the silent-stepping Birch cottage guest, her nephew Gavin came racing loudly to the beach, his older sister in tow.

Quickly slipping her laptop into her bag, she pushed to her feet and prepared for the onslaught. Within seconds she was wrapped in a loving embrace that filled her with joy. "Ooh, how I missed you."

Nowhere in her life would she have believed it possible to fall in love with two children so quickly. Yet, practically from the day her sister Iris had introduced Zinnia to Iris' two step-children, they had captured Zinnia's heart, and she couldn't imagine loving even her own children any more. If there was one pitfall to living and working in New York City and not seeing as much of her sister now that Iris lived on the lake, not being able to watch the kids growing and changing would be it.

Tucking each child under an arm, she turned to face her grandfather's newest guest. "Say hello to Mr. Ingram."

"How do you do?" her niece said. Followed by a more timid, "Hello," from her nephew.

David smiled. "Pleased to meet you."

"This is Gavin and Emily." From atop the hill, Iris came rushing down. Zinnia pointed in the breathless woman's direction. "And that is my sister, Iris."

"Sorry," Iris huffed. "I had my hands full with a box of modeling clay when they spotted you and took off. There was just enough time to hand it off to Lucy."

"Modeling clay?" Zinnia raised her hand to silence her sister before she could respond. "Let me guess. Grams?"

Iris nodded.

"Do you think she'll find anything she's really good at?"

"Everyone has a gift for something." Iris laughed. "I'm just not so sure it's in the arts and crafts arena for Grams or if she might have to wait till she gets to heaven."

"Amen to that." Zinnia rolled her eyes on a deep sigh.

"She paints very pretty rocks," Emily announced firmly in defense of her new great-grandmother.

"Yes, she does." Iris sidled up beside her step-daughter and kissed the top of her head. "She definitely does."

Zinnia squeezed her niece and nephew's shoulder and took a small step back. "Let's go see what Grams and the General are up to."

"Do you think Lucy made any peanut butter cookies today?" Gavin's eyes twinkled with enthusiasm.

"Maybe." Zinnia smiled. In actuality, she knew darn well that

Lucy always kept a fresh batch of the kid's favorite cookies and today was no exception. Turning a moment, she faced the man quietly watching the family interaction. "I should get back to the house. This time of day you might get better reception from the chair than I did, but just in case, I'll leave my beach towels here for you."

He glanced to the ground. The towels she'd been sitting on and huddled under in search of shade while working were rumpled but offered at least some protection between the sand and technology. "Thank you. Where shall I bring them when I'm done?"

"The main house. Or leave them here and someone will gather it up later on."

"I'll drop them off at Hart House when I'm done. Thank you. And again, I do apologize and promise to pay more attention from now on to where I'm going."

"And I promise not to huddle so far below eye level." She offered her best smile.

"Deal." He smiled back.

Halfway up the hill, her sister linked an elbow with Zinnia's as they followed the children already running up the front porch. "Care to explain what that was all about?"

"Nothing really. A lesson in watch where you're walking. Or working."

One eyebrow arched higher than the other a moment before Iris's brows dipped, forming a perfect V. "You sure about that?"

"Of course I am." After all, tumbling over a stranger wasn't indicative of anything more than the world's obsession with staying connected. That's all.

Taking a few seconds to glance over her shoulder at the shoreline, she had to admit, she wouldn't mind tumbling over that particular stranger.

CHAPTER FOUR

"**O**h my." Iris's nose lifted and sniffed at the air. "Corn bread?"

"Sure does smell like her honey sweet corn bread." One of the many things Zinnia had missed about being in Hart Land was the wonderful smells that came from the Hart family kitchen. She could make fun of Lucy's matchmaking from now till the next millennium, but the woman sure knew how to cook. And she wasn't a half bad baker either. Nothing like her cousin Lily, but Zinnia wouldn't turn away anything Lucy baked, and from the delicious aroma filling the front foyer, Zinnia didn't expect to be turning away today's treat either.

"There are my girls." Grams looked up from the table in the corner. A clump of clay sat to one side while Grams prodded at a spindly spike rising from the center of the table. To her other side, Gavin and Emily were in the final stages of tying on plastic aprons in bright primary colors.

"We're ready, Grams."

"Excellent." The silver haired woman, who looked as beautiful now as she had when Zinnia and Iris were little girls, leaned over to kiss each child on the cheek. Digging into the box Iris had dropped off, she pulled out a mound of clay in each hand and dropped them on the table in front of the children. "You can create whatever inspires you. If you need more, let me know."

"More?" Iris asked unsteadily, her gaze on the large blobs in front of them.

Grams lifted one shoulder nonchalantly and smiled at her granddaughter. "Some of the world's best masterpieces are much larger than life."

"Well." Iris stretched her hand out and snatched a peanut butter cookie from the top of the pile, handed it off to Zinnia, then took another for herself. "I say we try small scale for starters. You know, until they're old enough to be considered a master."

The intensity with which both children attacked their blobs made Zinnia want to smile. Neither cared about the adult banter, they simply wanted to create. As a kid she'd loved playing with modeling clay, Play-doh, or any other kind of hands on art project.

"We expected you to join us earlier." Grams returned to her own project. "After all, you're on vacation from that job of yours."

Zinnia spotted the twinkle in her grandmother's eyes seconds before the rest of the sentence came out.

"What is it you do again?" Grams didn't bother to look up. She had casual reconnaissance down pat.

"For a living," Lucy interjected, holding out a square of buttered corn bread on a paper plate.

"Oh, thank you." Zinnia reached for the proffered baked treat but her fingers hadn't quite connected with the still warm slice before Lucy yanked the plate back and handed it to Iris.

Brushing her hands off, Lucy slid the sharp knife into the bread once again. Carefully, she passed the slice onto another dish and held it up just out of Zinnia's reach. "You were saying about your job?"

"That's blackmail," Zinnia snapped.

"I think you mean bribery," Iris added on top of a slow moan. "Oh, Lucy. This is your best ever. Really."

Zinnia snapped her head around to face her sister. "Whose side are you on?"

"Me?" Iris shoved another morsel into her mouth and groaned again.

"You're killing me." She risked reaching for the paper plate. Pleased with herself for closing her grip on the proffered dish before Lucy could pull it away, Zinnia smiled up at the family housekeeper.

Lucy didn't ease her grip, she just waited for a response.

Blowing out a low sigh, Zinnia relaxed her shoulders. "I've already told you guys that I'm doing executive admin work, except now I get to pick and choose who I work for." Even if right now she only worked for one very demanding and well-paying client.

"Yes, you did." Grams nodded. "But I'm curious what sort of administrative work keeps you busy almost twenty-four seven?"

It took her a moment to gather her thoughts. The non-disclosure she signed prohibited her from sharing who she worked for or any personal knowledge of her boss, but that didn't mean she couldn't satisfy at least some of her family's curiosity. Besides, what little she said now wouldn't have an electronic paper trail like an email and she could be completely sure that no one had bugged her grandparents' house.

"I'm actually a private executive admin."

"Ooh, that sounds important," Lucy said with a grin.

Iris narrowed her gaze over the last piece of sweet corn bread she held in her hand. "Private executive?"

Zinnia nodded.

"So, you're buying the wife's gifts?"

"And wrapping them." Zinnia couldn't get in trouble for admitting that. Lots of once upon a time secretaries shopped for the gifts for their employer's wife. Though she wasn't thrilled with the way Iris was studying her.

"Are we talking Prada purse or diamond bracelet?"

"Prada was so last season," Zinnia teased, laughing the comment off.

"Ooh. Dropping chaff. So, both?"

Blast, this woman was good. A slow grin eased across Zinnia's lips. She really did love how smart her sister was. Iris had probably worked for a few families with more money than Croesus. If anyone understood the kind of people Zinnia worked for, it would be Iris.

"Maybe."

"Are we talking new or old money?" Iris continued her gentle prodding.

"What difference does it make?"

"To me?" Iris popped the last bite into her mouth and swallowed. "None, but you're the one who wanted to play twenty questions."

"I did not."

"Then just tell us. Who do you work for and why the need to be so secretive? Although," her sister waved a finger at her, "depending on who you work for, the why so secretive might be self explanatory. We've already established you don't work for a Mafioso." Iris stopped. "We did establish that, didn't we?"

Zinnia rolled her eyes skyward. "I do *not* work for a Mafioso."

"Good. Those guys can get tricky. Interesting code of honor. Usually protect women and children, but too easy to accidentally get caught in the crosshairs."

"And you know this how?" Grams stopped sculpting and stared at her granddaughter.

Iris shrugged. "I may have met one or two at a cocktail party."

"Well, I'm glad you don't go to those kinds of parties anymore." Grams returned her attention to the clay figure in front of her.

A dreamy look took over Iris' face as she uttered, "Me too." Though Zinnia was pretty sure the look had nothing to do with the mafia or the parties and everything to do with her new life in Hart Land.

"So," Iris turned to her sister, "you're not working for a mafia kingpin."

Zinnia refrained from rolling her eyes again and simply shook her head.

"But you are working for someone famous."

"I didn't say that."

"You didn't have to." Iris grinned. "I smell an NDA."

"I didn't say that either."

Her sister's grin widened. "Been there, done that. So, what can you tell us? Do you at least like your work?"

"Yes." That came out easily. She loved the work she did. A little crazy at times, but she really was enjoying it. Except. "Some days the hours are really long."

"Does he pay you well?"

"Better."

"That would explain it. The more money they have, the more they expect everyone to work as hard as they do."

"Some times I think harder." Heaven knew she'd spent enough time on her laptop after normal working hours in case Sam thought of something he might need from her.

"What's your favorite part, dear?" Grams asked without looking. Surely that tortured piece of clay was supposed to start looking like something. "Zinnia?"

"Oh, sorry, Grams. I was thinking."

"About what you enjoy most?"

"The art." She shrugged.

That caught her grandmother's attention. "Art?"

She nodded. "He's a collector of sorts. It's probably my favorite part of the job. From procurement to delivery, I get to keep tabs on it all."

"Oh, that does sound interesting," Grams said softly.

It was one of the perks of having generations of family money. Not only could Sam indulge every whim, whether traveling in private jets, buying another house, or adding a new Rembrandt to his collection, he also had more than enough left over to fuel the high cost of chasing a political career. And of course, pay for his privacy. Which brought her around full circle. Maybe keeping her business life under wraps here at Hart Land wasn't going to be as easy as she had once thought.

● ● ● ●

"I hear you had a challenging morning today." The General may have been retired for more years than any of his granddaughters had been working, but the man still carried an air of military authority that could not be denied.

"Yes, sir. You might say that, sir." David took a sip of water and reminded himself that he wasn't a raw recruit in the General's Marine Corps, he was a guest at the dinner table of his grandfather's friend.

"It took me a while to adapt to the lack of connectivity on the mountain." Zane, Callie's fiancé, shook his head lightly. "But we can always count on the wired connection for the closest thing to high speed the mountain has to offer."

"It's been out for days," Grams interjected with a smile. "How many days has it been, dear?"

The General looked to the ceiling. David could almost see him counting in his head. "Only three."

"Only?" Heather shook her head. "Feels like forever. The other day I actually had to hike up to Eagle's Point so I could get decent enough reception to respond to the backlog of emails I had."

"Why didn't you just go down to the beach like I did?" Zinnia asked.

"Maybe because I didn't want to be tripping over our guests."

"That's not fair. I didn't trip over him." Zinnia waved a thumb at David. "He tripped over me."

He considered apologizing for the umpteenth time, and settled for a contrite nod. "What's Eagle's Point?"

The granddaughter whose name he didn't recall, but he did remember she lived in Boston, set her knife down and turned to him. "It is the most peaceful and beautiful place on earth."

"I have to agree with Violet." The woman's husband nodded.

Violet. That was the granddaughter's name. David almost snapped his fingers. He was going to have to build a spreadsheet to keep track of who was who. At least he had one of the granddaughters' name etched in his memory. And a few other things about her. Even though no one could read his thoughts, he cleared his throat.

"I've been to a lot of places in this world," Violet's husband continued, "and the view from the top of Eagle's Point is hard to beat."

"What neither has said is that it's the highest point on this mountain," Zinnia provided. "It's been the heart of the family for generations."

"There's a great deal of sentimental value." Mrs. Hart's gaze met her husband's. For a few seconds the connection was so electrified, he could almost hear it sizzle.

His attention shifted to the other couples at the table. Everyone clearly seemed to understand something he was missing. Something much bigger than a mountain.

"Blueberry pie or Gargie's sponge cake?" Lucy, the famous matchmaking housekeeper, seemed to appear out of nowhere carrying a tray laden with desserts. She waited a split second for him to decide before adding, "Both are homemade."

It must've taken him longer than he thought to make up his mind because the General burst out in a loud chuckle. "Feel free to take both if you like."

His gaze snapped up to the older man. David's waistline needed two desserts like he needed a proverbial hole in the head. "Thank you. I think I'll try the blueberry pie." After all, he might be health-conscious but he wasn't stupid. Turning down homemade pie was akin to mortal sin in his family.

Chairs scraped against the floor as different family members moved about, some retrieving dinner dishes and carrying them into the kitchen, others filling glasses. Violet circled the table with a pot of coffee, and Heather the doctor followed behind Lucy, offering a scoop or two of ice cream to any takers. Within seconds the momentary mayhem had once again settled into a dinner time scene suitable for a Norman Rockwell portrait. The conversation easily shifted from the discussion of mountain tops and Internet connections to the upcoming wedding of the prominent heart surgeon.

Looking around the table, David was amazed at the size and diversity of this family. This particular weekend, Violet and her husband had come to visit in preparation for the upcoming nuptials. If he understood correctly, next weekend her sister Rose and her husband would be arriving, and by the end of the month the entire clan would be here for the big event.

"Will you be joining us for a session of cards this evening?" Mrs. Hart asked.

Stroking a dog at either side of him, the General spoke without looking up. "Your grandfather did teach you to play whist, did he not?"

"He did. But I'm afraid I'll have to pass tonight." He really should have passed on supper as well, but he suspected if Mrs. Hart had asked him in her sweet demeanor to jump naked into the icy lake, he would eagerly have complied as well.

"Oh, that is a shame." Lucy the housekeeper shrugged. "After a long day's work, an evening of family and fun is good for the soul. Are you sure you won't change your mind, even for one hand? I usually serve another round of pie for the card players."

The woman had no doubt noticed he practically inhaled her pie. And the offer was tempting. "I suppose—" The rest of his sentence gave way to a sharp pain in his leg.

From the seat beside him, Zinnia had kicked him. Hard. And she had the nerve to smile innocently at him. "I'm sure you'll have other evenings to play with us, won't you?"

For a smart man, it took him a few long seconds to put two and two together. The sweet smiling housekeeper had no doubt gone into matchmaking mode, and though he had no idea what she had up her sleeve, he and his aching leg were going to take Zinnia's advice.

Facing Lucy, he put on his best effort at a charming smile. "Thank you, but I really have to pass this evening. Maybe some other time."

The older woman's phone began playing the theme from *Hello Dolly* and it suddenly struck him that he might owe Zinnia a bigger debt of gratitude than he'd realized.

CHAPTER FIVE

"Now this is a cup of coffee." The first swallow of Zinnia's morning elixir was everything the fresh aroma had promised.

Heather lifted her own mug at her cousin in a mock toast. "If only I could get Lucy to make coffee for the doctor's lounge at the new hospital. It would make all of our lives so much more pleasant."

"I daresay, wars could be won if leaders would only sit across the table with a cup of Lucy's coffee." Grams pushed to her feet, carrying her empty cup to the buffet for a refill.

"As a general of the United States Marine Corps, I can honestly attest that your grandmother is absolutely correct."

Every pair of eyes of the room swung around to stare at the General. The man had to be getting soft in his old age. There is no way on this green earth that he would have agreed to any such comment. Not even from the woman he adored.

Grams detoured around the table behind her husband, patting him gently on the shoulder and leaning in for a tender kiss on the cheek. "You know darn well I was embellishing, but it is ever so sweet of you to have agreed."

Her grandfather's thick, large hands engulfed her grandmother's smaller ones. The bright light in his eyes and the soft smile on his lips told everyone in the room that for the woman he had loved for over 60 years, he would have gladly agreed the world was flat.

"Who is taking our latest guest his breakfast?" Lucy entered the dining room carrying a covered tray.

"Don't look at me." Poppy wiped her mouth with a napkin and pushed away from the table. "I promised the pastor I'd be at church early this morning to help the youth counselor prepare for the annual lock-in."

Heather shook her head. "I have a conference call in fifteen minutes with a new candidate for my team."

"Then I guess that leaves you, dear." Grams settled into her seat at the opposite end of the table.

Since technically there was no reason for Zinnia to have to check in with her only client this morning, she was free and clear to play room service staff. "Sure. No problem."

"Be sure to knock really loud in case he's still sleeping." Lucy handed off the tray.

"Still sleeping? Why does he want breakfast if he's still sleeping?"

Lucy shrugged. "He didn't exactly order it. But if he's not going to make it up here to eat with everybody else, then the least I can do is make sure he gets a good meal to start his day."

"But what if he wants to sleep in?" She didn't mind helping out, but dragging a person out of bed first thing in the morning, especially if this is supposed to be a vacation, was not top ten on her hit parade of favorite things to do after only having time to consume one cup of coffee.

"Nonsense." Lucy waved off her concerns. "There isn't a guest on this mountain who would want to sleep in instead of having my blueberry pancakes with real maple syrup, Katie's home-churned butter, crisp bacon, local eggs, and of course, fresh pastries from Lily's."

Considering how little the man had eaten last night, Zinnia was fairly sure that Lucy was overfeeding him for breakfast, but when it came to picking battles this was not the hill that she was willing to die on. Like it or not, Mr. Ingram would be having breakfast served hopefully not in bed.

Halfway down the hill to the Birch cottage, she could see movement through the windows. At least she wouldn't have to worry about waking him up. Hopefully, he wasn't already cooking his own breakfast. On the front porch, carefully juggling the tray with one hand, she gently knocked at the door.

"Coming," carried gently through the yellow hardwood portal.

Unexpected anticipation had her taking a step back, and quickly controlling the jiggling tray with two hands.

The door flung open, and the bare-chested man with sleep tousled hair blinked at her. Twice. "Good morning." David's gravelly early morning voice was deep and hot enough to melt a pan of frozen butter, and maybe her knees.

Lifting up the tray, she plastered on a casual grin. "Lucy thought you might like a hot breakfast."

Long fingers raked through his unkempt hair and settled behind his neck. Closing one eye, he tipped his head at her. "I don't suppose that breakfast includes hot coffee? I can't seem to get the coffeemaker to work."

"As a matter of fact," she grinned up at him, "an entire carafe."

"Is it too early in the relationship to ask Lucy to marry me?" He nudged the door open a little wider and reached for the tray.

"I can honestly say, you're not the first man to say that. Wait till you taste the pancakes." She released her hold on the breakfast.

Easing back, he glanced toward the small kitchen and back at her. "Would you care to join me?"

Not wanting to scream yes like an anxious teen, she took a moment to reply. "I might as well save you the trip of returning the tray."

He nodded and tipped his head for her to follow him inside. Setting the tray down on the table, he took a deep whiff of the hot coffee and sighed. She knew how he felt. "Will you have a cup?" He waved at the tall carafe. "This is more than even I'll drink."

"I never turn down a cup of Lucy's coffee."

"That good?" He looked down at the table and seemed to notice his own navel. "Excuse me. I'll be right back."

"I'll pour the coffee," she called over her shoulder en route to the cupboard where the cups were kept. There wasn't much to learning where thing were kept. All cottages had similar layouts and the stocked cabinets had a system the General had established before she was born. "Do you use cream or sugar?"

"Black," he called from down the hall as he reappeared, tugging a t-shirt down over his head. "Thank you."

"My pleasure."

Both hands swaddling the warm mug, he swallowed his first sip. "Oh, this is just what I needed."

"Does seem to get the day off on the right foot."

Leaning back in the chair, he took another long slow sip and almost sighed. "If I were a cat I'd be purring."

That made Zinnia laugh. She knew exactly what he meant. The first day she'd returned to the lake after being away for so long, she could have sat on the porch, rocking, enjoying the view, and inhaling Lucy's coffee for hours.

He set the cup on the table and reached for a pancake. "I suspect that I owe you thanks for last night."

Last night? She couldn't put her finger on anything she'd done out of the ordinary.

"The card game." It wasn't a question. "I got the impression, at least after you kicked me, that there was more to the game than a deck of cards."

Of course. "At the time I didn't know who, but I could tell by the look in Lucy's eye that she had something up her sleeve, and that something involved you."

"Really? You can tell by the gleam in someone's eye?"

"Yep. My cousins, who spend more time here at the lake, are even better at it than I am. Through the years it gets easier to recognize Lucy's tells. Turns out, surprise surprise, Louise's granddaughter is visiting for the weekend from Boston."

He broke off a piece of bread and buttered it. "Not the usual suspect?"

"Nope." Zinnia shook her head. "But she does have a string of bad relationships behind her. One of which I didn't even know had ended. According to Lucy, all she really needs is to meet the right man."

David's head dipped in a single affirmative motion. "And that would be me?"

"Now you're catching on."

"And how would she know I'm the right man?"

"All she has to know is that you are gainfully employed, legally unattached, and if you happen to have a streak of military respect…" she let her words trail off a moment. "I gather from your efforts to get online that you do have a job. A rather demanding one at that."

"Law school professor, and legal consultant."

"Consultant?"

"Expert witness. Occasional advisement. That sort of thing."

"Oh, I can see Lucy working on the balance sheet now. Lucky for you, the granddaughter goes home tonight."

David chuckled softly. "I'd like to think I'm more than just a spreadsheet of numbers."

Indulging herself, she let her gaze travel from his twinkling eyes to his strong chin and broad shoulders. Definitely more than a spreadsheet.

● ● ● ●

When David had first woken up this morning and quickly discovered the coffee pot was not cooperating, he thought for sure it was an omen of the kind of day he was going to have. Turns out it was anything but. Enjoying a homemade breakfast with Zinnia was successfully exceeding any of his anticipations for his stay at the lake. Heck, who was he kidding, enjoying breakfast with her would be the highlight of pretty much any day, anywhere.

Had he body slammed any other woman on a beach anywhere else in the world, he'd probably be battered and bruised, at least with words if not actions, and would have deserved it. Instead she'd been mostly amused by the ridiculousness of the whole slapstick episode. Then last night, watching the family at dinner, listening to the lilt of her voice, the silly stories about her and her sisters had him totally intrigued. He nudged the pastry dish in her direction. "You haven't touched anything."

"I already ate at the house. Let's just say that I have a weak spot for Lucy's blueberry pancakes."

"How about lunch?" he blurted out.

She turned her wrist to check the time. "A little early for lunch, don't you think? Besides, you should be full by now."

Way to go, Professor. How to sound like an idiot 101. "What I should have said was that I'd like to take you to lunch. Call it a proper thank you."

"For what?"

"Okay. Make that a proper apology for stumbling over you yesterday."

"Another apology isn't necessary, but lunch would be nice."

"It would?" He sounded more surprised than he'd intended.

That same amused smile from yesterday, after she'd taken in the situation, teased at the corner of her lips. "Are you asking me or telling me?"

Once again, he'd successfully opened mouth and inserted foot. This was crazy. He wasn't a naïve teen. His profession required eloquence. So why did she have him so flummoxed? "Telling you."

"Did you have any place in particular in mind?"

"No. Do you have a preference?"

"Despite how small we are, there are a lot of options. From Mabel's Diner all the way to the steakhouse across the lake." She hesitated a moment. "Although…"

"Although what?"

"This may sound a bit odd, but there's a grocery and bait shop for this side of the mountain, and it's recently opened for lunch."

"A bait shop?" He didn't need a mirror to know his eyes were wide as a startled owl.

"Yes, but the bait's not on the menu. At least not for the people. I've heard that she recently put a few tables outside and is serving up a light lunch. Though I'm not sure if there's anything more than lobster roll on the menu."

"Lobster roll?" They were close enough to Maine lobster country for his mouth to practically start watering.

"Yes," she chuckled. "Best this side of the bay."

"Which bay?"

"Any bay."

"Sold." He had no idea what he was getting into, but he was willing to take a risk. Besides, there'd be no faulting the company. Bait shop lunch it would be.

CHAPTER SIX

"Ooh. What have we got here?" Zinnia set the dirty dishes in the sink and hurried over to where Heather, Violet and Cindy sat at the table.

"They're out of champagne-colored tablecloths." Heather flipped through a large binder with pages of different colored fabrics.

"How does that happen?" Bending her knee underneath her, she half sat, half leaned on the table.

"Apparently the industrial strength dryer the launderer uses caught fire." Cindy lifted a pale yellow swatch, shook her head and put it back.

"And I presume," she shifted her gaze to her cousin, "everything in it?"

Cindy pressed her fingertip to her nose. "Give the girl a prize."

"Can't they just get new ones?" Violet unfolded her legs from beneath her.

"They can. And they will. Just not by the wedding date." Heather pulled out a dark blood red fabric. "Maybe I should just turn direction completely."

"Or maybe you should ask your wedding coordinator. Isn't that what she's for?" Zinnia fingered the vibrant toned fabric.

"Wedding coordinator?" Violet looked up. "With my mother, the queen of the party scene on hand?"

"Well, yes, but still."

All of her cousins stared at her as if she had never before met her own aunt.

"Okay. Maybe you have a point. But what about the actual wedding? Is Aunt Becky planning on running all over the church and reception putting out fires? Sorry," Zinnia held up her hand, "not literally."

"Understood." Heather bobbed her head. "And for that we have a Day-Of coordinator. Even though it's actually the *week of.* I thought it might be easier to just pick a color and tell Mom, but now I'm beginning to see where it's a blasted game of dominoes. The tablecloths affect everything in the room, from the candles and flowers to the bar front and seat cushions."

"It's really not that hard." Zinnia pulled out two coordinating fabrics. "If you use these, you can still have the dusty rose-colored flowers in the centerpieces. You won't even have to layer with a table topper. This deep blue will make the dishes and charger plates stand out and it will go very nicely with the mauve bridesmaid colors."

"She has a point." Cindy stepped back and with one eye closed, studied the fabric swatches. "It would make the tables pop a bit more. Not quite so dull."

"Dull?" Heather almost whined. "You think my tables were going to be dull?"

"Of course not. I'm just saying." Cindy paused, then turned to Zinnia. "Tell her what I mean, Zin."

Bless the great veterinarian. A regular Dr. Doolittle with the animals. Not so much with the humans. "She just means it will make as lovely a contrasting shade as the original golden champagne and white you and Aunt Becky had originally chosen."

"Oh, I hope so. I have no idea why out of all of us I got the straw for the biggest and most complicated wedding." Heather heaved a sigh and stared at the swatch Zinnia had handed her. "But I do think you're right. I'll let the caterer tell Mom."

"Thatta girl." Zinnia shoulder bumped her cousin. "When in doubt, delegate."

Heather smiled at her cousin and shook her head. "If only all of life were this easy. So now, tell me where you learned about coordinating tablecloths? And don't tell me it was watching my mother."

"You could say I've had to help with a few fundraisers."

"Rose?" Cindy asked.

Zinnia shook her head. "My main client."

"You have more than one?"

It took a moment to decide how to answer that. Technically she had more than one, she just only worked for one. "Yes, but at the moment I'm only contracted to work with the one who likes his privacy."

"Ooh." Violet grinned. "It's a he."

"Who's a he?" Grams walked into the room.

"No one," Zinnia answered quickly as Cindy and Violet echoed, "Her boss."

Grams smiled sweetly from one granddaughter to the other. "I see."

And she probably did. Grams was the sweetest smart woman Zinnia had ever known. That woman said so much with her smiling eyes.

Hauling eggs from the backup fridge, Lucy came in grinning. "I heard that. Is he married?"

"Yes." Finally a question that Zinnia didn't feel guilty answering. At least fifty percent of the adult male population had to be married. She wasn't giving anything away by revealing that one small detail.

The way the family housekeeper's shoulders dropped, anyone would have thought someone had stuck a pin in her to let the air out.

"Good morning." Coming through the kitchen doorway, Iris strode straight to the coffee pot. "Hey, Zin. Did you see the latest piece Kathleen Regatta is working on?"

Zinnia shook her head. She hadn't had much time for reading lately. It was her intention to catch up during her time in Hart Land.

"It's a doozy. Behind the scenes on the Gambini family."

"Who are the Gambinis?" Lucy piled the ingredients for home made gravy on the counter.

"Ooh. What are we having for supper?" Iris asked.

"Chicken cutlets parmesan, and who are the Gambinis?" Lucy persisted.

"No one special." Violet reached for an apple. "Just one of the most famous mob families on the East Coast."

"I've got a better question." Heather spun around to face Zinnia. "*Who* is Kathleen Regatta?"

"My best friend in high school. Even though she went to college upstate and I stayed in the city, we still stayed pretty close."

"I think I remember her." Cindy narrowed her gaze in thought. "About your height. Dark curly hair. Thin. Great tan. Her favorite swimsuit was yellow with red polka dots?"

"Yep. That's Kat." Zinnia smiled.

"If you barely remember her, how do you know that was her favorite swimsuit?" Iris asked.

"Elementary, my dear Watson. In all the years she'd come to the lake, she always wore that same suit."

"That would do it," Iris agreed.

"I really need to make some time to give her a call, it's been too long." Zinnia pushed to her feet. "And on that note, I've got a few errands to run. Anyone need something in town?"

Several heads turned from side to side.

"If you're anywhere near Katie's, I could use some of her fresh basil," Lucy said.

"Basil. Got it." Zinnia casually made her way to the front door, thrilled to escape without revealing she was having lunch with a man. Not that it mattered what man. For Lucy, the words opposite sex and matrimony went together like bagels and cream cheese. "See you later."

A few more steps and she crossed the threshold, almost gleeful when the door latched shut behind her. Bounding down the porch steps, she hurried to her car and calculated she had about ten to fifteen minutes before someone from the house needed to look out a window or step out of the house. Ten to fifteen minutes to collect her lunch date and escape to Katie's.

Her hand fisted, primed to knock on the door, the wooden entry swung open.

"Sure I will. No problem. You're welcome." David waved her in with one hand and dropped the handle for the landline into its cradle. "That was your grandmother."

"Grams? What did she need?"

"For me to ask you to also pick up oregano while we're at Katie's."

"Oregano." She sighed. "Got it." And apparently so did her grandmother. Some days she really wondered if that sweet, silent powerhouse could read minds.

"Oh, and can we make a stop at the dump?" His nose crinkled.

"No trash pickup here. Looks like we're taking the scenic route to lunch." At least she could be sure of one thing; the detour had nothing to do with Lucy and her matchmaking.

• • • •

"I have to admit," David hefted the last black garbage bag into the back of the General's Jeep, "I've been to some interesting places, but this may be my first ever visit to a dump."

Zinnia smothered a smile. "And I bet you thought all this lovely mountain had to offer was a beautiful lake, gorgeous trees, and restful views."

"Silly me." He slid into the passenger seat and clicked the safety belt. Earlier, when he'd considered the different things he might be able to do on the mountain, or places he might go with Zinnia, or anyone else for that matter, the county dump had not been anywhere near his radar, never mind on it.

At the top of the hill, Zinnia turned right onto the main road away from town. "The road to the dump is about halfway to where we're going."

A few minutes down the road and she slowed the vehicle then turned left, crossing the pavement and up a narrow dirt path. He hesitated to call the thing a road. One more pothole and he feared the Jeep might lose a wheel or two. "Wouldn't it make sense to pave this?"

Zinnia shrugged. "I guess they figure folks will drive slower if they have to maneuver around the potholes."

She rounded the bend and drove through an open double gate. The place looked pretty much the way he might expect. In the distance were several hills of colored and discolored goods. Slightly to the right of the main hills, a smaller pile of discarded furnishings almost reminded him of a country flea market. "In a pinch a person could decorate an apartment from here."

"Don't think it hasn't been done." Zinnia laughed. "That's why they're not put in the main trash hill. The dump is very recycling conscious."

He followed her to a small, dark red cabin with dusty white trim situated about halfway between the gate and the larger hills of trash.

The bottom half of the front door was closed and the upper Dutch style door remained wide open.

"Henry," Zinnia called as she reached for the handle. "Yoo hoo."

No answer.

"That's odd." She walked into the small office and repeated Henry's name. Still no answer. "Usually if he has to leave, he locks the main gate."

"Maybe it was an emergency? Or perhaps he's outside doing whatever dump people do with mounds of garbage."

"Perhaps. I suppose we can get the trash out of the Jeep. We don't really need Henry to sort it out. Lucy and the General are beyond diligent about separating glass from paper and compostables from ordinary garbage, though Henry likes to double check everything that comes through the gate."

"Sounds like a dream job." He smiled to soften the edge of his words.

A bag in each hand, he looked up at her. "Where to?"

"Behind the cabin is the triage area."

"Triage?"

She shrugged. "What can I say? Henry takes his job very seriously."

Leading the way around the cabin, he came to a stop. "Oh, isn't that cute."

"Cute?" Zinnia came up beside him and stopped short. "Uh oh."

Behind the cabin a small outdoor living area had been set up. The old sofa, coffee table, and loveseat were organized into a seating space unlike the other scattered discarded furnishings he'd seen when they'd first arrived. He could only assume that Henry liked to sit outdoors on occasion. Though the stench riding the wind from time to time made it seem less then an appealing alternative to inside the closed cabin.

"This can't be good."

"They're cute." Sitting with his feet straight out and leaning against the sofa back, like any little kid, the cutest bear cub batted arms with his sibling. Neither had paid any attention to his and Zinnia's arrival. "I'm sure if we don't bother them, they won't bother us."

Slowly her head inched around to face him. "You don't know much about bears, do you?"

"I know enough to keep my distance. But these guys are small and otherwise entertained."

"First rule of living in the mountains with bears. Where there are cubs, somewhere close there's going to be a mama."

"Mama?" He hadn't considered that. This wouldn't be the first time he'd heard such a thing, but the two little ones were so cute, he'd not thought about the repercussions.

Zinnia nodded. "Slowly put the bags down. I suggest we get ourselves back to the Jeep and do another dump run later when Henry's here."

No sooner had they released their grips on the large black bags then a heart-stopping roar sent shivers down his spine and the hairs on the nape of his neck stood on end. Sure enough, standing upright, arms in the air, halfway between the cabin and the Jeep, Mama made herself known.

"Or not," Zinnia mumbled.

Mama waved an arm and roared again. At this point he hoped to heaven Papa wasn't anywhere close by. Wouldn't that just be the cherry on their lunch plans?

CHAPTER SEVEN

In all the years Zinnia had spent her summers on the mountain, or time visiting her grandparents, why did today have to be the only time she ran into bears.

"Now what?" Without moving an inch, David spoke very softly.

At least she had to be thankful she wasn't with a city girlfriend. The last thing she needed was a startled female to screech. Or worse, run. "On our side, she just wants to protect the cubs and we're not really close to them yet."

"And we can't go far, she's standing in front of the car."

"True, but if we move out of her way, she should go to be with her cubs."

"Get out of her way?" Eyes open even wider than moments ago and speaking softly so the bear wouldn't hear, David's gaze bounced from the cubs to the bear to the Jeep and back. "I'm all ears. What do you suggest?"

"Well. According to everything my grandfather has ever told me," she said quietly, "never turn your back."

David nodded silently.

"Don't scream or make any loud noises."

Now he cast a quick glance in her direction, his gaze doubtful, but he nodded anyway.

"Speak in a soft and reassuring tone."

"To me or the bear?"

She knew he was just trying to keep the situation impossibly light, but she answered anyway. "The bear."

"Whatever you say."

"It's okay, Mama," she spoke clearly to the bear but not too loudly. "We're not going to hurt your babies." Still staring the bear in the eye, she whispered to David through the side of her mouth, "If we move left, away from the cubs and the cabin, she'll be slow to follow. Low center of gravity or some such thing."

David nodded and followed her slow movement to the side. So far, so good. She repeated the same soothing phrase. Never taking her eyes away from Mama, then dared another step to the left. Then another. The bear hadn't moved toward her cubs yet, but she hadn't come after them yet either. That was a very good thing.

"I think it's working," David murmured almost too quietly to hear.

Out of nowhere, Henry appeared at the front gate behind the bear, cradling a large brown bag. When he spotted Zinnia and David frozen in a staring contest with the big brown bear, his eyes rounded wide as an owl on steroids.

Zinnia dared to continue her sideways motion, her heart beating faster with every step. Why wasn't the bear moving toward her cubs?

"Should we try stepping back?" David whispered.

"Maybe." At least if it was the wrong move, Henry was here to call for help.

But help was already on the way. On the other side of the fence she could see her cousin Cindy driving up. The bear seemed suddenly aware of Henry behind her and let out another roar that made Zinnia cringe.

Now that Mama had spotted Henry, he went ahead and threw some of the contents to the other side of the cabin en route to the cubs.

Whatever Mama had been thinking, the thought of easy food seemed more appealing. Slowly, she moved forward toward the tossed food.

Zinnia wasn't sure exactly when it happened, but she found her hand firmly gripped in David's. He nudged her to continue inching toward the Jeep in a wide circle away from the bear. She wasn't completely sure which was more reassuring, her cousin holding a rifle pointed at Mama, or the warmth of David's hand squeezing hers.

A few more minutes and Mama and the cubs were happily chomping on grapefruits, allowing Zinnia and David to hop in the Jeep and make a beeline for the gate.

"I didn't want to lock them inside," Henry said. "I was hoping they'd be back up the mountain by the time I got back with some food to bait her away with."

Zinnia nodded. Her heart was still banging away too fast for her to find enough air to form words.

"You okay, honey?" Cindy still held the rifle with one hand and placed her other hand on Zinnia's forehead.

"I'm fine now. Thanks. You weren't going to shoot her, were you?"

"Only tranquilize if I needed to." Her cousin's hand checked Zinnia's pulse. Apparently satisfied, she nodded. "Why don't you two get out of here? The fewer people hanging around the gate the more likely Mama and her little ones will go home." She must have understood the hesitation on Zinnia's part. "We'll be fine. Remember," she held up the rifle, "I've got the fire power."

"I suppose when you put it that way…" Zinnia let her words fall off.

About to shift gears and drive away, she realized once again her hand was safe and warm in David's. Needing to pull away to get the Jeep moving forward, she just hoped she wouldn't have to come face to face with another bear for him to do that again.

● ● ● ●

The cell phone in Zinnia's purse vibrated and buzzed.

"Would you check that for me please? It could be Cindy."

Under normal circumstances David made it a point never to read other people's text messages for any reason. He'd been a lawyer far too long, and seen how something so simple could go terribly wrong in a court of law. But he was concerned for Cindy, and Henry as well.

As his mind processed the words, a tension eased from his chest. "Mama and cubs are waddling off into the trees." He flipped her phone to show her. "She sent a photo."

Zinnia glanced over and smiled. "That's a relief. I didn't like leaving them there, but I had to remind myself that my cousin has been handling situations like this for years."

"Is dealing with bears typical veterinary work in this part of the country?"

"Not usually, but Cindy is the only animal expert for miles. She does all sorts of calls for the sheriff's department. I'm sure bears have come up before. Probably more than once or twice."

He dropped her phone into the empty space on the console.

"I wonder how they got them out of the dump?"

"Carefully."

"Ha ha." She smiled.

"Sorry. Since the bear wasn't tranquilized, either she got tired of all the people at the dump, or she followed Henry's trail of food."

"My money's on the food."

Zinnia nodded and pulled into the gravel lot to the side of the road. David's gaze traveled from the tall trees ahead to the dock below, over to the few scattered tables to the side and lastly, to the large One Stop sign. "Where does it say this is a bait shop?"

"There." Zinnia slipped into an unmarked parking spot, pointing to a bait sign at the top of the dock ramp.

"I see the sign." Quickly he ran over his brief visit with the nice Irish lady and couldn't for the life of him remember anything that reminded him of bait. "But don't remember any bait inside."

"That's because there isn't." Out of the car, Zinnia rested her forearms on the roof and peered over the top of the car at him. "Who would want bait and food in the same room?"

That particular thought had crossed his mind.

Zinnia pushed back from the car and smiled. "There's a little shop—a shack really—between where boats dock and the store."

"I see." He followed her into the One Stop, his gaze mostly on the small red shack he'd spotted off to the side. On the front door hung a lopsided sign that sloppily read: Gone Fishing.

"What's so funny?" Zinnia asked.

He shook his head and reached for the door handle. "Nothing really."

"Why don't I believe you?"

"It was the sign." He lifted his chin, pointing in the direction of the bait shack.

Zinnia smiled. "Katie has a great sense of humor."

"Well, if it isn't our own Miss Zinnia. What brings you to our humble neck of the woods?" Katie finished bagging a few groceries for the person in front of the checkout counter. "Surely you can't be here for Heather's wedding already?"

"I could and I am." She flashed a bright smile that made him want to smile too.

"Isn't that a bit of good news! You work so hard. About time that boss gave you some time off. Now, what brings you here?"

"Two of your lobster rolls and a couple of pops." Zinnia turned to him. "Is that okay?"

He nodded.

"You go on and have a seat outside and I'll have your lunch to you in a jiff."

"Oh. And I'll have some oregano for Lucy."

Katie bobbed her head. "Will do."

Once again, David held the door for her and followed her outside and then around the corner.

"It's not much. If you want we could go back to Hart House?"

"No." He shook his head. "This is perfect. Good food. Good views. Good company. What more could a man ask for?"

"I suppose it depends on the man." Again, that bright smile lit up her face.

Holding her chair out for her, he waited till she was seated to straddle his own seat, and leaning his arms across the back, set his chin down on his hands and watched the sight before him. "Tell me about this job that keeps you so busy?"

"You too?" She sighed, then held up her hand. "Sorry. Everyone keeps peppering me with questions and guesses about my job."

He didn't need to be hit over the head with a sledgehammer to know the lady preferred her privacy. "Fair enough."

Her gaze on the lake in the distance, she smiled. "It's no big deal. I'm a private executive assistant to a gentleman in New York City."

"Could be nice. Except it sounds like he's a workaholic."

"Most ambitious people are to some extent, but it is a very nice job. Occasionally high stress, usually a lot of hours, but always pleasant atmosphere and great pay." Her gaze twinkled at the sight of Katie carrying out a tray laden with their lunch.

"I'm out of regular pop so one of you gets orange. Is that a problem?"

Both of them twisted their head from side to side.

"Good. Just whistle if you need anything else."

David was pretty sure his eyes were popping out of his head. The overflowing sandwich in front of him was a sight to behold. The sandwich firmly gripped in his hands, he leaned forward and took a big bite. As if orchestrated, he and Zinnia moaned their delight simultaneously. "Okay. This is by far the best lobster roll I have ever had. Even better than Maine."

"Agreed." Zinnia took another bite.

"The lobster itself is nice and sweet but there's something else."

"We think it's Katie's secret mayonnaise recipe. Which, since it doesn't taste like mayo, it must be some other secret sauce."

"Whatever it is, I wouldn't mind buying a bottle or ten." It did his heart good to see Zinnia chuckle at his attempt at humor.

"You and everyone on this mountain." She set her sandwich down on the paper plate, licked a dab of sauce from her thumb, and tipped her head at him. "Have you been able to get any work done?"

"Not enough. As much as I love the law, it's hard to write about it when everywhere I look, the lake is sparkling with invitation." The spotty cell phone service wasn't helping anyhow. On top of the blasted article hanging over his head, he'd hoped to hear an update from Jason by now, but the lack of cell signal was not on his side.

"I know what you mean about the lake. Some days she's like a siren's song. Did you always want to be a lawyer?"

He felt his cheeks tugging his lips into a smile. "Does any little boy want to grow up and be a lawyer?"

"Let me guess." Eyes narrowed, she studied him a long few minutes. "Baseball player?"

"Nope."

Wiping her hands on the paper napkin, she kept her gaze on him. "Any sport?"

He shook his head.

"Then it has to be fireman."

"Has to be?"

"Doesn't every little boy want to be either a sports star or fireman?"

"Maybe." He shrugged. "But I wanted to be a rock star."

"A musician." Her brows rose again but this time her eyes reflected admiration not surprise. "What instrument do you play?"

"And that would be why I went to law school. Not only did I dislike my piano teacher and my guitar teacher, by the time my voice changed it was clear to anyone within listening distance that I couldn't carry a tune with a forklift."

She chuckled softly. "Then I guess it's a good thing you had law school for a backup plan."

"That's what my grandfather says. Though he'd rather I'd gone into the JAG Corps."

"Military lawyer." She nodded. "I could see that."

"Career military are a lot like married people. Once they're signed up for life they think everyone else should be too."

Having just taken a sip of her drink, she sputtered, and covering her face, swallowed hard. Half coughing and half laughing, she sputtered some more. "Sorry, I'd not heard that before."

"And you know what they say?"

Lightly patting her chest to stop the coughing, she focused her beautiful blue eyes on him. "What would that be?"

"The closer to reality, the funnier the commentary."

"Ain't that the truth. But never any interest in the military?"

He shook his head. "I did one stint in a tough as Marines summer camp and knew beyond the shadow of any doubt I was not meant to rise with the roosters or follow orders."

"Few people are. Then again, not everyone is cut out for law school either."

"That sounds like the voice of experience."

"Law briefly made it to my list of career opportunities but by the end of my senior year of college the thought of even one more exam, never mind three more years worth, was about as appealing as jumping from an airplane without a parachute."

"I guess just jumping from an airplane wasn't off-putting enough?"

She laughed. "Let's just say I'd have rather skydived than gone back to school."

"No regrets?"

"Not a one. I love my work." Her smile continued to light up her whole face.

"It shows. So, what did little Zinnia want to be when she grew up?"

"You mean before a lawyer?" She grinned at him. "I inherited my mother's sense of rhythm."

"Oh. So you wanted to be a ballerina?"

"Not exactly." She kept grinning at him. "I thought a stripper might be more lucrative."

He shouldn't have had that last sip. Expecting something more mundane like a pianist or music teacher, he almost spewed his drink all over her and the last morsels of their lunch. Over the immediate shock of the startling response, he had to wonder, how many more surprises did this woman have in store for him?

CHAPTER EIGHT

"I can't believe the bears picked today of all days to hang out at the dump." Seated by her grandfather in the large dining room at Hart House, Cindy stabbed at the last bits of food on her plate.

Zinnia was thinking more or less the same thing. Not anything extraordinary about today, but she could've done without the extra excitement. Though she was pleased, at least for a short while, to have been holding hands with David. It had been so long since she'd had the time to spend with friends, never mind date, not that lunch had been a date. But whatever it was, she liked it.

"I'm still struggling with the idea that my very competent and capable wife spent the afternoon with a family of bears." Cindy's husband Alan held out an empty plate.

"Better your wife than mine." Violet's husband Grant patted his wife's hand.

Violet grinned up at him. "Amen to that. I may have crossed paths with some crotchety people in desperate need of a little relaxation, but I for one am not interested in calming a true savage beast."

Scooping a portion of Lucy's cobbler onto her husband's plate, Cindy shook her head. "It wasn't an entire family, only a mama and her cubs."

"Oh, well." Violet chuckled and rolled her eyes.

Alan waved a fork at Violet. "I'm with your cousin here. How exactly does that make a difference?"

"Knock, knock," Louise Franklin mimicked the sound of her knuckles rapping on the doorframe.

"Just in time for dessert." Grams waved the family friend and many-a-night card player into the room.

"I know I'm early but I wanted to find out all the nitty-gritty details from the horse's mouth. So to speak." She smiled at Cindy.

"There's no nitty or gritty." Cindy sliced into her dessert.

"Of course there is." Louise grabbed a nearby chair and pulled it up to the table. "According to Betty when she popped into the pharmacy for some of her allergy meds. This year's allergy season simply doesn't seem to want to go away. Anyhow, she mentioned Zinnia and some man had been trapped at the dump by a bear."

"Well, maybe not trapped exactly," Zinnia chimed in. After all, there was a good chance they probably would have made it out on their own if the cavalry hadn't arrived.

Hands on her hips, Louise spun around to face Zinnia. "Was there or was there not a bear between you and your car?"

She couldn't very well argue that point. "Yes, there was a bear at the dump."

"See?" Louise spun back to face Cindy. "Mabel said—"

"Mabel?" Poppy's face crinkled in confusion. "What happened to Betty?"

Louise waved her off. "She could barely stop sneezing long enough to tell me that Henry had called for reinforcements."

"Did I miss anything?" Thelma hurried into the dining room and came to a screeching halt in front of David's chair. "Oh, my. You must be the handsome man trapped with Zinnia and the three bears?"

"That sounds too much like a nursery rhyme for a deadly situation." Louise rolled her eyes at her dearest friend.

Thelma ignored the commentary and extended her hand to David. "I'm Thelma Carson."

"David Ingram," he responded, his gaze shifting from Thelma to Louise and back. "A pleasure to meet you."

Thelma's lips lifted in a soft smile, but the glint in her eyes was almost predatory. "I assure you the pleasure is all mine."

"Put your eyes back in your head, Thelma." Louise shook her head.

Thelma ambled away, grabbing another chair and mumbling there was no harm in looking.

Before she could get settled, Ralph came marching through the doorway. "For two people almost mauled to death by three angry bears, you guys look pretty good to me."

"Am I to presume since you're eating dessert now, we don't

need more for the card game?" Lucy stood staring at the empty cobbler dish.

"I'm sure this is fine, Lucy. Thank you." Louise pointed at the dish in front of her and then waved the same finger at Cindy. "So tell us, how did you get rid of the bears?"

"I thought I'd find you here." Floyd the barber stood in the doorway.

Holding the empty dessert dish in her hands, Lucy moved past Floyd muttering, "Good thing we keep extra in this house."

"I didn't do anything." Cindy let her fork rest on the dish. "Though I was prepared, Zinnia and David had eased far enough away that the mama bear lost interest in them as a threat to her cubs."

"Mama bear?" The General stopped petting his dog and leaned forward. "No one said anything about a mama bear before."

"It's fine, sir. We weren't that close really." Zinnia supposed it would be too much to ask for word about the incident not to get all around town.

"So now that we're all good and curious," Grams dabbed at the corners of her mouth, "how did all of you get the bears to go away?"

"Henry called me and then ran over to Katie's to get some fruit and food for the animals. Once they noticed he had tossed edibles out of reach, the bear moved far enough away that Zinnia and David could make a break for the Jeep."

"I admit," Zinnia smiled at her cousin, "I am a little curious myself as to how you got her cubs to leave."

"That part was easy. Once you and David were safely out of the compound area, like the witch in Hansel and Gretel, Henry dumped the rest of the fruit making a trail along the perimeter, through the gate, and slightly out to get him enough room to close the gates. Which he did the minute Mama and both cubs were outside."

"Easy peasy," Grams said with a smile.

It definitely might sound that way now safely seated with family and friends, but at the time, it sure hadn't felt that way.

• • • •

Following the conversation like a foursome tennis match was more entertainment than David would have expected from a sleepy lake family. He really was enjoying his stay more than he'd expected. He might have only been here a couple of days, but they were full days.

His breast pocket vibrated, reminding him his phone was actually turned on.

"Don't look so surprised," the General chuckled. "It works from time to time. Just not as predictably as any of us would like."

"If you'll excuse me." He pushed away from the table and phone to his ear, hurried to the outside porch and down the front steps. "David here."

"We've got a problem." Even with no preamble, he recognized this client's voice.

Some days it drove him absolutely nuts when people used the royal *we*. This evening was definitely one of those days. "You'd better make it quick, I'm not sure how long my reception will last."

"Tell me about it. I've been trying to call you since yesterday afternoon."

For the next few minutes he listened to a client who consulted with him for his expert advice more and more often of late. Not that the man didn't have enough lawyers of his own, but this particular client was the sort who had to double and triple check everything and the more expensive the advice, the more likely he'd be to believe it. The man prattled on for another long few minutes when David spotted the group from inside gathering on the porch. "I really have to go. There's only one way to know what's fact and what's conjecture, and talking off the record isn't the answer. I'll call Al—your lead attorney," not that the guy didn't know who the lawyer actually on retainer was, "and see what he's doing about this."

The voices on the porch got louder and David broke free of the call. Overhead, the whirl of a helicopter caught his attention. "Why would anyone need a helicopter up here?"

"Probably going to the big house on the other side of town." He hadn't heard Zinnia come up behind him.

"Makes sense in Manhattan where it takes longer to find a parking space than to walk across town, but up here." He shrugged. "Seems like overkill."

"Probably, but so is the big house. It makes Hart House look like a summer cottage."

"Really? Who does it belong to?"

"We're not sure. It was just recently sold. We thought some rich family from Connecticut, I think. Or maybe it was New Jersey. I don't remember exactly. But the only one seen coming or going is a woman. She seems to have a lot of guests. From what Katie tells Grams, I'm pretty sure the guests are up here more than she is. The staff does all the ordering and I don't think a single person in town has actually met anyone."

"Seems a shame to be up here where everyone is so friendly and be so…unfriendly."

She shrugged. "Their loss."

That's exactly what he was thinking. Granted, the crowd this evening was rather entertaining. He paused and looked up at the house. "Are those two really named Thelma and Louise?"

"Yep. And they've been friends since long before the movie." One side of her mouth tipped upward in a sly grin. "They say the truth is stranger than fiction. With those two, I wouldn't be surprised."

That made him chuckle. He'd learned a long time ago never to underestimate two older women on a mission. As a matter of fact, if he had his druthers, he couldn't think of anyone better to have on his side if he ever got in trouble than a pair of feisty old women. Still he'd make it a point to stay away from convertibles when with them.

"You two joining us?" Floyd called down from the porch.

"Joining them?"

"Cards," Zinnia reminded him. "Whist."

"That's right." Taking a moment, he glanced down the hill toward his cabin and the beach. Why did connecting to the outside world have to be so difficult here?

As if following his thoughts, Zinnia let out a soft sigh. "Were you able to get at least some work done since lunch?"

"*Some.*" He didn't want to tell her that connectivity hadn't mattered much since he'd been unable to focus on anything other than her anyhow. At this rate, if he continued to spend more time with Zinnia and the Harts than his computer and upcoming deadline, the internet would be the least of his troubles.

• • • •

"He is a good looking fellow." Lucy stood beside Fiona, looking over her shoulder.

"He is." The one Fiona was more interested in watching was her husband. Bantering with Floyd and Ralph over music on Main Street this summer, he kept a hand scratching the top of each dog's head, and an eye on David and Zinnia. That man was up to something.

"Martha is frustrated with Lawson." Lucy stepped back and waved her hand at Fiona. "Don't get me wrong. I'm not saying she's right. This town has been home since I was old enough to ride a tricycle and I love every inch of it and the people in it."

"But…" Fiona coaxed.

"I do understand why young people want to get out and live a little. Martha has big city fever. Combine it with man fever and it can be a dangerous thing. Unless we can find her the right man."

"We? You got a mouse in your pocket?"

Lucy grinned and Fiona had this funny feeling that her housekeeper and friend just might have something up her sleeve.

With all the granddaughters getting married, the daughters remodeling, and great-grandchildren arriving on the scene, Fiona wasn't sure she had it in her to deal with whatever Lucy had in mind. "Lucy."

"What?" That who-me grin was a dangerous thing. "We both agree he seems like a very nice man."

"I don't think he'll be here long enough for Martha to get to know him, if that's what you're thinking."

"Maybe." Lucy grinned again.

Glancing over at her husband, Fiona caught him watching Zinnia and his school buddy's grandson coming up the walkway. She was going to have to give this whole grandsons and granddaughters thing a little thought.

Lady, one of the General's golden retrievers, came trotting up to her, sat at her side, and seemed to follow the couple as they climbed the porch steps. As the door opened the dog gave a small whimper and the next thing Fiona knew the two dogs were running circles around the human's feet. David and Zinnia couldn't have been more entangled if they'd been a couple of skeins of yarn at the bottom of a knitting basket.

A small bark of triumph and Sarge returned to his master's side and Lady came to once again sit by Fiona. If she didn't know better she'd swear the old dog was smiling up at her. "Et tu, Lady? Et tu?"

CHAPTER NINE

"Blast." Heather came hopping out of her room, advancing down the hall on one foot while slipping her shoe onto the other and then visa versa. "Why don't emergencies ever happen in the middle of the day?"

At this hour of the morning, Zinnia had only intended to use the little girls' room and then slide back under the covers and catch another couple of hours of beauty sleep. The last couple of nights she had been up late—or early, depending on how a person looked at it—participating in the ritual card games. It was difficult to explain to a stranger why for someone growing up on the lake, the card games had held so much appeal. And apparently based on her lack of beauty sleep, still did.

Last night had been especially entertaining—and late—with David joining the clan. The guy was not only handsome, smart, and full of interesting stories, he could hold his own against the General at cards, and *that* said a lot about a man. Bumping into her cousin had left her suddenly very wide awake and tossing her plans to sleep in out the window. "Emergency?"

Heather nodded. "An accident up the mountain. Little girl was found under a rock slide."

"Oh no." She didn't like the sound of that at all.

"They got to her in time and thought she was doing just fine, but now she's presenting with a list of symptoms I don't like including myocardial ischemia."

"Myocardial what?"

"Blood flow to the heart is reduced, preventing the heart muscle from receiving enough oxygen."

"Oh."

"I need a favor."

"Want a ride?" Zinnia turned back to her room to grab her car keys. Shoes and real clothes could wait.

"No, thanks. Can you call Kelly at the florist and tell her what happened? See if you can pick up the sample centerpieces she made and bring them here. I'll look at them when I get a chance."

"Sure." Zinnia followed her cousin down the steps.

Heather was already at the front door. "Thanks. I'm sure they'll look fine, but Kelly won't move forward without my approval."

"Can't say that I blame her." Zinnia took in a deep breath. "Keep us posted on the little girl."

"Will do!" Heather trotted down the steps and into her car.

"What's all the commotion?" A dog on either side of him, the General came out from his study.

"Heather was called out on an emergency."

Their grandfather shook his head. "Never a good way to start the morning."

"No." Her gaze lingered on the empty parking spot Heather had pulled away from. "Not at all."

"My, my, we're all up bright and early." Grams came up beside Zinnia and gave her a soft kiss on the temple and a gentle one-armed squeeze. Somehow her grandmother always seemed to know when a little extra comfort was called for. And now was one of those times. Zinnia had no idea who the injured little girl was, and yet her heart ached for the child nonetheless.

Leaning into her grandmother's side, Zinnia took in a deep breath of lilacs and vanilla. She loved the gentle scent of her Gram's perfume. Slowly they made their way into the kitchen. Even at this hour of the morning, Lucy already had command of the large kitchen. Smells of warm pastry competed with the soothing scents of lilac and vanilla. But the thing that most had Zinnia's attention was the enticing aroma of fresh brewed coffee.

"I thought I heard an awful lot of footsteps for this hour." Lucy smiled at Zinnia and held out an already filled mug, then glanced over Zinnia's shoulder. "Aren't we missing someone?"

"Heather." Zinnia slowly swallowed the first fortifying jolt of soothing coffee. "She got called into work."

"Work?" Lucy's forehead folded in confusion. "The only work she's supposed to be doing is getting ready to get married."

"A little girl was hurt."

"Oh, no." Lucy's hands lifted to her heart.

Zinnia raised her hand. "I know, but I figure with the best cardiac surgeon on the eastern seaboard—"

"Country," her grandmother proudly corrected.

"Country," Zinnia agreed, "hurrying to take care of whatever ails her, the little girl is already on the best track to recovery."

Lucy let out a slow long breath and nodded.

"So. Today I get to do fill in for Heather and pick up the samples from the florist."

"You're deciding on the centerpieces?"

"No. Just picking them up for Heather to see whenever she gets home. But I will admit I'm kind of excited to have a sort of important part in all this. With me not being able to come up to the lake very often, there hasn't been much I could do."

"I'm sure she appreciates that you're able to do this for her." Grams put a kettle of water on the stove.

"I know."

Lucy turned toward the refrigerator. "Since you're up early enough to choose, would you like pancakes or French toast?"

That was an easy one. Zinnia would take Lucy's French toast over just about any breakfast food. "Stuffed?"

Lucy grinned. "Is there any other way? As a matter of fact," she set an extra dozen eggs on the island, "I think I'll make extra for David. The poor man was such a good sport at the card game last night."

"Poor man?" Zinnia held back a chuckle. "He won almost every hand."

"I know, but he was partnered with Thelma. Surprised the woman didn't drool on her cards."

"Now Lucy," Grams chided sweetly.

"Don't you now Lucy me. Thelma was in fine form last night. David seems to bring out the… shall we say more interesting side of her."

"That and a few glasses of Pinot." Grams chuckled. "I'd better go join your grandfather in the dining room. He does enjoy a good cup of coffee with his newspaper."

"Some days I think he's the last man left in the state who still reads his news on paper."

"He's not the only one." David came into the kitchen and smiled at Lucy. "I saw Heather pull out and thought that might mean the coffee is brewing."

"Always," Lucy responded with a smile. From what Zinnia could see, Thelma wasn't the only one taken with David. "You guys join the General and Miss Fiona in the dining room. I'll bring the coffee."

"Can I help with something?" David asked.

If Lucy wasn't taken with him already, she was hooked now. "I suppose you can take the coffee pot out and I'll get started on the French toast."

"Is the table set?" Zinnia knew the answer, usually Lucy set it after supper in case the General beat her to the breakfast table in the morning.

"It is. Now get going."

She followed David across the hall. By the time they were seated, Poppy had joined them. Zinnia was going to miss the mornings with her cousins when it was time to go home. Already with Violet and her husband back in Boston, the table seemed a little empty.

"You're up awfully early." Poppy poured herself some coffee and slid into her regular seat.

"I heard Heather and didn't see any point in going back to bed."

"Heather?" As though she could see the through the ceiling, Poppy glanced up.

"There was an emergency, but I'm sure all will be fine." Grams stirred her tea.

"In the meantime, I'm going into town to pick up some centerpieces for her to choose from."

"Pick up? Wouldn't a photograph do?"

Zinnia shrugged. "No idea. I'm just doing as I'm told. Want to come with me?"

"Can't." Poppy shook her head. "I'm alone at the church office today and don't dare leave. You know if I did that would be the minute the church would catch on fire or elders would ride down Main Street in their birthday suits."

"Now that's a vision I didn't need to see." The General

shuddered. "And what are your plans for the day, David?"

"I should do some work, but I'm beginning to believe that work might have to wait until I'm home."

"Excellent idea. Life's too short to spend all of it working. Believe me, I know."

"Yes, sir. I'm sure you do."

"Perhaps you could accompany my granddaughter. In case she needs help with her charge."

"I'd be glad to." He turned to face her. "If you don't mind?"

"Not at all." She couldn't think of anyone else she'd want to be confined with in the close quarters of a motor vehicle. Hopefully no bears would show up this time.

• • • •

"I'm afraid this little jaunt is going to be a bit boring."

The other day they had turned right to go to the dump. Now, Zinnia turned in the opposite direction and followed Main Street toward the center of town.

"I've heard wonderful things about Lawford. This will be my chance to see for myself." David gladly would have followed her around no matter how boring the prospects.

"So this is you first visit to downtown Lawford?"

"Only if driving down Main Street on my way to the lake house doesn't count."

"Most definitely not. A person can't get the flavor of a place without stopping to enjoy." She slowed the car. "For instance, did you notice the old-fashioned barber pole?"

Had he? On his arrival the other day he'd been more focused on his destination than the journey. "Don't think I did."

Her finger waved off to the side and now he did remember noticing the old pole when he came in. "We also have Betty's. If you want a traditional wash and set, she's your girl."

Though he could see from the sign that Betty's was a human hair salon, the question still seemed more appropriate for a poodle. "Wash and set?"

"Ever see an old movie where the women are gossiping away

while sitting under hair dryers that look like space aliens?"

"Let me guess. After having their hair washed and set in the dryer?"

"Well, actually, they were set with curlers. But yes. That would be the result."

"And some people still want this?"

"Mostly my grandmother's generation."

"Traditional." The word held a great deal more meaning driving down Main Street than it might in midtown Manhattan. As Zinnia pointed each shop out, he took in the old bookstore, the hardware store, the funeral parlor—owned by her aunt—the ice cream shop that had him suddenly craving a dark fudge banana split from his childhood, and finally, the flower shop. Or at least, he hoped that's what Kabloom was.

Flanked by colorful blooms to either side, the bright pink door beckoned all guests to step inside. The garden-fresh aroma of cut flowers slapped David in the face and made him smile.

"Come on in." David wasn't sure what he expected the shopkeeper to be for a postcard perfect shop, but the perky blonde was definitely not it. In her early twenties at the most, with hair down to her waist and a broad grin that remained intact as she handled a stoic customer, she seemed the personification of a happy spring flower.

"You'll see to it that they are delivered by the end of day to all three addresses."

"Not a problem," the woman chirped gleefully. "We have a very reliable network we work with."

"Very well." The man turned on his heel, took one step and froze when his gaze met Zinnia's.

David couldn't blame the guy. The young clerk was attractive in a co-ed sort of way, but Zinnia was a knockout. Her blue eyes sparkled, her smile warmed a man deep in his soul, and the sleek navy dress that subtly hid other assets shouted class act.

"Zinnia?" The man arched a brow.

Zinnia spun about and raised both her brows in surprise. "Oh. Hello."

Something about the guy seemed terribly familiar, but David couldn't put his finger on it. And whatever it was, had warning bells dinging in the back of his mind. He simply didn't like the way the guy's expression warmed at the sight of Zinnia. Not that David had a right to be jealous. *Jealous*? Was that what was prickling at him? How crazy was that. Even after only a few days at the lake, the draw to this woman was stronger than anyone he'd ever known. *That* he'd be an idiot to deny. But jealous?

Another of his consulting clients set his phone off and he knew if he didn't take the call now, he might not be able to talk again for who knew how long. "I need to answer this. I'll take it outside."

Zinnia nodded at him as he hurried out the door.

One eye on the two people talking inside, he listened to the ranting client on the other end of the phone. The last thing he wanted was to listen to this man prattle on. Giving his full attention to a client should have been a priority. Attention to detail was key in legal representation. His reputation for not allowing the slightest detail to slip by was known far and wide. Too bad the only detail he wanted to pay attention to was Zinnia relaxing and smiling with a man who rubbed him the wrong way—and there wasn't a thing he could do about.

● ● ● ●

"This really is a surprise." It took Zinnia a couple of beats to put a place and name to the face and then it suddenly struck her. Her boss's brother, Charlie.

"A little far from Manhattan." The man had a smile as captivating as his brother. Though they shared few similar features, that high wattage grin and brooding dark eyes were two valuable assets. At least with the three women the guy was sending flowers to. She could only hope it was his wife and mother and maybe a sister she knew nothing about. "Are you passing through?"

"Oh, no. I grew up spending summers on this lake. Now I'm back for my cousin's wedding."

"Excellent reason." He smiled and the gruff expression of a few minutes ago slid away. "Weddings hold so much promise. My wife tells me I'm a sentimental fool, but I do enjoy seeing young love blossom."

"That's very sweet. Are you staying nearby?"

He nodded. "I am. With a…friend."

"If you're going to be here till the end of the month, you should let me know. It's quite the shindig. Practically the whole mountain is invited. Scratch that. The whole mountain has to be on that guest list. It's longer than I am."

Charlie laughed. "Sounds like a big deal indeed."

"If you love weddings as much as you say, you and your friend should join us. The whole town will be there. It would be a great chance for your friend to meet the neighbors."

A somber expression briefly veiled previously smiling eyes. She wasn't sure what the deal was with this guy. She remembered the day he showed up at work to see Sam. She'd spent about fifteen or twenty minutes chatting with him until Sam showed up. The conversation had centered mostly on her unique name and how her mother and aunts had come to name all their daughters after flowers. She hadn't given it much thought at the time, but she'd actually learned very little about him other than to see simmering fury in Sam's eyes when he'd found his brother waiting in his office.

At the time she'd wondered what could have driven siblings so far apart that one would blow a gasket if the other showed up at his workplace. She couldn't imagine anything but joy if Violet or Heather were to turn up. Even though she wasn't supposed to share where she worked, she still wouldn't have reacted like Sam had.

The tension seemed to slip from Charlie's features. "That's very generous of you, but I don't expect to be here that long." He took a step back. "I'd better be on my way. It was nice bumping into you. Give my regards to Sam."

"Will do." Resisting the urge to mention he should call his own brother himself, her gaze remained on the man's departing back. He nodded to David as he passed him on the sidewalk and disappeared down Main Street. What kind of falling out had the two brothers had? She just might have to try and do something about that—whatever it was.

CHAPTER TEN

"**I**'m certainly not a wedding expert, but these look pretty nice to me. I would never have realized they weren't real." Taking the larger centerpiece from Zinnia's arms, David loaded the last sample into the back of the Jeep.

"It's going to be a lovely wedding." Brushing her hands together, Zinnia turned to him and smiled. It really was a very nice smile.

Opening the driver side door for her, he took a step back.

Zinnia flipped her wrist to see the time. "That took a little longer than I expected."

His phone call with Al, his cranky client's attorney, who had ignored his legal opinion on what steps to take to shut down an unpleasant situation and was now eager to close the barn door after the horse had already gotten out, and Zinnia's encounter with someone she clearly hadn't seen in a long while, had easily increased the length of their quick errand with the extroverted florist. "Kelly seems very nice."

"She is. But she can definitely be quite the talker. It's best not to stop in if you're in a hurry."

"But we're not in a hurry." At least he wasn't, regardless of stubborn clients who keep secrets, their equally stubborn lawyers, and the barrage of phone calls that would no doubt be forthcoming. He certainly hoped she wasn't in any hurry either. "Now where to?"

Her smile brightened. "What would you like to see of our fair town?"

You was probably not an appropriate answer. The truth was he didn't care where they went right now. He was just delighted that she wasn't in a hurry to return to work. As long as he got a chance to spend some more time with just her, she could show him anything in town she wanted. Even another visit with the Bear family. "What do you suggest?"

"Have you had any luck with your hotspot signal?"

He shrugged. "That depends on what you consider luck."

"Have you been able to get your work finished?"

Now was also not the appropriate time to tell her his lack of productivity had much less to do with his lack of connectivity and more to do with his interest in spending time near her. Even if it meant playing cards with the infamous Thelma and Louise. Now that was a pair he wouldn't mind a little more background on. Then again, he couldn't be held responsible in a court of law for something he didn't know. He had to bite back a smile, something he was doing an awful lot of lately. "Not even close to getting my work done."

She bobbed her head. "Then there's only one choice. We'll pop into the One Stop and grab a couple of sandwiches."

"And then?"

Her eyes crinkled with amusement. "You'll see."

Ha. Another side to the many facets of Zinnia Colby.

"Give me a minute to check in with the house and see if Heather is back yet." Phone in hand, Zinnia hit speaker and listened to the ringing of a phone on the other end.

"Doesn't it drive you nuts that sometimes a call goes through and sometimes it doesn't?"

She shook her head. "It's just a fact of life up here. Besides, in this case, I'm calling the house landline so I know I'll be able to get through."

In a minute, someone picked up. Zinnia dispensed with some minor chitchat before asking about Heather and her patient, then nodding and smiling, sprinkled with a few *I see* and *okays*, followed by an *I love you too*, she disconnected the call. "The good news is her patient is going to be just fine, but she wants to stay at the hospital to make sure there are no surprises."

"That sounds like a dedicated doctor."

Repositioning her sunglasses atop her head, she leveled her gaze with his. "A damn good dedicated doctor."

"Agreed."

"Since Heather won't be home for a while, we don't need to make a pit stop to drop off the baskets."

"Makes sense."

She slid her glasses onto the bridge of her nose and slapping her hands together, rubbed them enthusiastically. "Are you ready?"

He had no idea if the playful side to this woman was going to be a good or bad thing, but right now he was more than willing to simply enjoy the ride. "Ready."

• • • •

"I have to admit, if I lived here," David held up the large sack Katie had packed with their lunch from the One Stop, "I would stop at Katie's every day for one—or two—of her lobster rolls. Even if it meant being buried some day in a piano case."

"You and everyone in town. We're all trying to figure out what her secret is. Though there's always a chance she has leprechauns working under that counter of hers." She might've been teasing when she said it, but some days Zinnia and the rest of this town wondered if indeed Katie wasn't surrounded by leprechauns or some other magical Irish fairies.

At the narrow dirt road not far from the Hart Land main entrance, she turned right up the bumpy hill. "Hang on to those sandwiches."

Gripping the door handle as the front wheels sank into a deep dip and bounced him up, David clenched the bag in his other arm. "Guarding these babies with my life."

The two laughed harder with every jolt and bump until Zinnia pulled to a slight clearing, threw the stick shift into neutral and pulled on the parking brake. "We walk the rest of the way."

His gaze lifted from the bag in his arm up the narrow wooded path. She had no idea what thoughts were running through his mind, but with a curt nod he waved his free arm upward with just a hint of flourish. "After you, milady."

Such a simple turn of phrase, a common gesture, and he had her smiling once again. Since their first encounter by the lake he'd had her smiling so often, her cheeks almost hurt. They'd only progressed a few yards when Zinnia tripped over a root and losing her footing, wobbled backward.

Immediately, David dropped their lunch and lunged forward, grabbing hold of her before she could tumble down the hill. "Are you okay?"

"Sorry about that. I've been up this hill a million times, even in the dark, and I don't ever remember making such a rookie misstep." Of course not one of those million times had she been up here with David, or anyone she was especially eager to share their family's treasured view with.

Slowly easing his hands away from her, remaining close enough to grab her if she wobbled again, he gave a lazy shrug. "We all have our moments. You sure you're okay?"

She seriously contemplated accidentally slipping again just to feel the strength of his hands around her waist, but common sense took root. Blast her common sense. "Yes."

"Onward then." David leaned over to pick up their lunch bag.

Pointing to the bag held in his arm again, she hefted her other hand on her hip. "I thought you were going to guard that with your life?"

His eyes twinkled with merriment, a huge grin spread from ear to ear. "I lied."

Resisting the urge to grab hold of her hand with every step, after a short slow hike of only a few more minutes, he found himself standing at the top of what was now clearly a mountain.

"Amazing, isn't it?"

Overlooking the magnificent valley and lake below, he snapped his mouth shut and nodded. Amazing didn't even begin to cover it.

"Shall we have a seat?"

Silently he stepped around the large carved log that served as a bench for anyone who cared to take the time and appreciate nature's artistry. "I considered myself a reasonably well-traveled person."

She nodded.

"But this tops anything I've seen."

"We all know how lucky we are that some relative generations ago didn't give into the almighty dollar and sell this land."

"Amen to that." So taken with the silence and the beauty, both of the view before him and the woman sitting beside him, he hadn't noticed when she'd taken the bag and removed their sandwiches and drinks until the famous wrapped lobster roll dangled in front of his face. "Thank you. I almost forgot I was hungry."

She couldn't explain why, but his reaction meant more to her than it should have. This place had been special to every Hart descendent since Jeremiah carved his bride's name all those hundreds of years ago. It made her heart happy to see him appreciate it as much as they did.

"You mentioned before that you don't get away from New York often."

"That's right." She took a bite.

"I think if I'd grown up with all of this at my disposal I'd find a way to come back."

"I say that every time I do come and then I return to New York, get sucked into the rat race and the next thing I know…"

"Yeah. What is that old expression: Life is what happens while we're busy making other plans."

"Exactly."

David's gaze settled on a distant point. "I need to spend more time with my grandfather. Spending time with yours reminds me how much I enjoy being around him. Even if he can bounce a quarter on his bedsheets."

That made Zinnia laugh. She understood exactly how he felt. As a kid growing up there were some days that she expected a bugle to blow and everyone in the house to be out on the front lawn doing calisthenics. Fortunately, the one thing her grandfather adored more than the Marine Corps had a more practical perspective on life. Grams gave the General the balance their family needed. And Zinnia loved them both with everything she had in her.

"I was probably only five years old when he taught me how to play cards. I was a whiz at poker by the time I was six, and soon after was introduced to the joys of Whist."

"I don't remember a time we didn't play whist." She crumpled the empty sandwich wrapper into a ball and dropped it in the paper sack. "I was always a bit too impulsive to truly master the game. Don't get me wrong. I can play, but some of my cousins are better suited for the strategy. I just see a lot of one suit and want that kitty at any cost. Often to my partner's chagrin."

"I'll partner with you any time." The tenderness of his smile warmed her down to her toes. Now she knew why so many romance books declared the hero's smile should be registered as a lethal weapon. She could see herself agreeing to anything the man behind that smile asked.

"This was a great place for lunch." He tossed his trash into the brown bag. "Thanks for sharing with me."

"My pleasure, but I actually had another reason besides the view for bringing you up here."

"Really?" One eyebrow shot up high on his forehead and she almost spit out the sip of pop she'd barely swallowed.

She twisted the cap on the bottle and hoped her cheeks weren't flushing bright pink. "The last thing anyone who comes up here wants to do is connect with the outside world, but the reception up here is phenomenal."

His gaze skimmed one side of the mountain and stopped at her. "A lot of things up here are phenomenal."

• • • •

If given a choice, Zinnia would have gladly spent the entire afternoon sitting on Eagle's Point chatting with David. Exchanging stories of growing up with a military grandfather, with someone who truly understood the two sides of a senior officer, the regulation-heavy uniform on the outside and the marshmallow on the inside, somehow made the memories all the sweeter.

It didn't take long to set the centerpieces up in the parlor. With Heather expected home shortly, along with her cousins joining them for dinner, Zinnia anticipated another fun evening of last minute wedding plans. Not that they had much left to plan. At this point just about every thing had been decided and Zinnia was a tad surprised the centerpiece choice was still up in the air. No matter which ones Heather chose, this was going to be one heck of a wedding.

Poppy fingered one of the displays. "I say use them all."

"I don't know." Heather stared at the options. "Something doesn't feel right."

"They're flowers." Iris glanced at her cousin. "What's to feel?"

"Is there a rule book on flowers that I'm missing?" Lily passed around a dish of her latest test treat.

"Ooh. These are good." Poppy reached for another. "What are they?"

"Don't know. Haven't thought up a name yet."

"Well, whatever you call them, I vote them keepers." Poppy practically hummed with delight. "And I still think the centerpieces are all pretty."

"But she's right," Zinnia spoke up. "This one in the candy dish-looking thing on a pedestal has a slightly more formal look to it than the other two. Even though the wood bowl and the tin box are different materials, they're still more casual."

"That's it!" Heather smiled. "But I love the flower colors and arrangement."

"So," Iris shrugged, "we tell Kelly to change out the candy dish to some other container that works with that arrangement."

"And voila, problem solved. Arrangements finished. And we're done." Iris pushed to her feet.

"Not so fast." Heather flashed a toothy grin and Iris flopped back in her seat. "We need to fill these."

"What are these?" Poppy peered her nose into one of the boxes Heather pointed to.

"Those are the rose-colored mesh bags for the hot cocoa packets." Heather whirled her finger to point at a different box. "And those are the blue mesh bags for the coffee."

Violet stared up at her cousin. "Coffee and cocoa?"

"Favors. Except first we have to affix these," she lifted a smaller box beside her, "to each packet."

Iris pulled out a stack of labels that read *The Perfect Blend* and held one up. "How many?"

"Only five hundred."

"Five hundred!" Poppy almost spit out the wine she'd just sipped.

"Each."

"Good heavens." Iris peered into the other packet of labels. "How many people are invited?"

"Two hundred and fifty, but Grams thought it would be a nice touch to let folks take more than one if they wanted."

"She's right." Zinnia lifted one of the tie back bags. "Kind of a cute idea."

"Glad you like it." Heather smiled. "We ordered them so long ago, I'd almost forgotten about them."

Zinnia's phone dinged. She'd gotten so used to a silent phone that the sound had her jumping off her seat. Scrolling through the alerts, she found the most recent. "Oh, hell."

"What is it?" Poppy asked mid bite. That was her fourth treat, but who was counting.

Scrolling to another screen then another, she blew out a deep sigh. "The delivery company on a recent purchase I made for my boss is delivering to the wrong address."

"Oh no. Where?" Iris came to stand over her shoulder.

"My apartment."

Poppy came to stand on her other side. "Why is that wrong?"

"Because no one is there to receive it. It was supposed to be delivered to my boss's home in Connecticut."

"So tell them to re-route."

"I'm working on it." Zinnia really would have preferred her laptop for this, but with the still dead internet and spotty hot spot, she'd lose valuable time connecting. The last thing she needed now was a mad dash jaunt to New York. Blast.

CHAPTER ELEVEN

Sleeping in, no matter how late he'd gone to bed, was a concept that had always eluded him. Though in college and law school, the ability to function with little or no sleep had served him well. Since arriving at the lake, sleeping in had come surprisingly easily, until this morning. Though he didn't mind. Enjoying a hot cup of coffee on the porch of his little cabin was a peaceful start to the day.

If he were honest with himself, he would have to admit that any start to the day would be a peaceful one if it started on Lake Lawford. Maybe General Hart could keep an eye out for some nearby lake property. Never too early to plan for retirement, and his grandfather would probably love having the opportunity to visit his academy buddy. From the conversations the last few evenings it sounded like Mrs. Hart and his grandmother had more than enough in common to be good friends. After all, how many people plan to vacation together if they don't get along? Though he did wonder why his grandfather hadn't said anything about an academy reunion and reconnecting with buddies he'd lost touch with, like General Hart.

In just a bit it would be time to pop up to the Hart house for breakfast. He tried not to arrive too early as Zinnia was not an early riser and she was the star attraction. Not that Lucy's cooking wouldn't win over any man's heart, but Zinnia reminded a man of why he didn't live by bread alone.

The morning sun sparkled against the water, the coffee cup warmed his hands, and his mind wandered back over Zinnia and the last few days. The only reason he'd accepted his grandfather's suggestion to work from the lake was one of practicality. Change of scenery was always a good idea to help stimulate fresh ideas. The thing he hadn't banked on was finding someone considerably more interesting than any responsibility or deadline.

"I was hoping you'd be up," Zinnia's voice carried from behind his shoulder, as she moved around to stand before him.

"Good morning."

"Morning." Her gaze drifted off toward the shoreline and he wondered what thoughts danced around in her head when she spied the lake on an early morning.

He lifted his cup in the air. "Would you like one?"

"Wish I could." She blew out a slow breath and turned to face him. "I have to take a run into New York."

If the look on her face was to be believed, this wouldn't be a welcome jaunt. "Nothing serious, I hope."

"Only if you consider human error serious."

"Okay."

"Sorry. I'm just annoyed that I have to go all the way into the city to sign for a package and then wait around all day to turn it around to where it should have been delivered in the first place."

"That does seem to be a bit of a nuisance."

She blinked and nodded. "I'm hopeful that the delivery service will pick it up in time for me to come back to the lake tonight, but I'm not going to hold my breath."

"Would you like company?" He wasn't sure where that had come from. Normally, the last thing he usually wanted to do was be stuck in a car with someone for five hours twice in a single day. Then again, nothing that involved Zinnia seemed to fall into his definition of normally. "I mean, it's a long drive." Oh brother. Now she was not only turning his normal reactions on their head, she had him tongue tied and stupid too. Some litigator. "I mean—"

A warm smile touched her lips. "I know what you mean. I hate to put you up to that. It's a lot of driving."

"Time goes by much faster if you have company."

She nodded. "If you mean it."

"I do."

"Thanks."

"Give me five minutes to shower and I'll be ready to go."

"Have you had breakfast yet?"

He shook his head.

"I'll grab something to go from the house and meet you by the car."

"You got it." His gaze lingered on her retreating back longer than it probably should have, but it was a nice back. Turning on his heel and hurrying inside, it occurred to him that driving into Manhattan hadn't held this much appeal since he was a kid on a field trip from the suburbs to the Statue of Liberty.

"You don't mind my car, do you? It's not as big as yours."

"I don't mind at all, but we can take mine if you prefer?" For whatever reason he wouldn't mind if they rode tandem on a bicycle.

"As long as you don't mind the smaller car, I'd feel better putting the added wear and tear on my car."

"Whatever the lady wants." Waving an arm, he stood by the hood of her car, bowed at the waist then lifted his chin to grin at her. Pleased with the small chuckle of a response, he snapped upright and opened her door for her.

Halfway to Manhattan, they'd been chatting pretty much non-stop.

"I honestly had no idea all that was involved in pulling off a wedding." David tugged on the seatbelt and shifted. "It's rather mind boggling. The family makes it sound like despite the trappings it's really more of an oversized family barbecue." Though he wasn't so sure of the last analogy. Whoever heard of a 250 person family barbecue.

"This is the most involved I've been on any of the weddings."

"Your grandfather slipped me an invitation last night after the card game. I felt like a kid passing notes in school." He couldn't imagine what it was and then was rather surprised to find it was an invitation to the wedding. And even more surprising for him was that from the moment he realized he was welcome, he very much wanted to accept. "I've been thinking I might be able to extend my visit till then."

"Really?" Her voice lifted in what he hoped was happy surprise.

"I'm not that big a fan of weddings in general, but for some reason I feel like I have a stake in this one."

"Well." Zinnia straightened her shoulders and if he wasn't mistaken, her grip on the wheel seemed to tighten. "When you put it that way," she chuckled, "since we were both in on the flower caper, then I guess we both have a stake that this comes off as planned. We should go together. You know. Keep an eye on each other's interest."

"Absolutely," in a heartbeat he eagerly accepted. If she'd meant the invite to be a gag, the gag was on her because he intended to escort her in style.

• • • •

When Zinnia learned that the only way to resolve the problem with the delivery of the statue from the auction house was to accept delivery and then order a totally separate pickup and redelivery, she'd almost cried. For some insane reason it was considered a security risk to allow the original delivery to be moved, but not a risk to order a second delivery. Of course, for all she knew it had nothing to do with security and everything to do with the almighty dollar and being double charged, but the way Sam spent money on famous artwork, she doubted the delivery fees mattered for anything.

Nothing about driving into the city and losing a day with David and her family held even the tiniest of appeal. Until now. The last five hours had flown by. Learning he would be staying at the lake not just for a couple more days but until the wedding had made her day. Having him accept her rambling invitation was the icing on the cake. Before she realized it, she'd turned onto the FDR Drive and depending on traffic, was only a few minutes from her place. "You were right."

"Thank you." He grinned. "What about?"

Silly comebacks like this one had been the sort of thing to keep her smiling and laughing most of the drive. "The ride goes faster with company."

"Ah." He leaned back in the seat and kept his gaze upward on the buildings they passed. "We really do live in a unique place."

"We do," she agreed. Two more blocks and she turned into a parking garage then glanced at the dashboard clock. The transport company had given her a two hour window for delivery. "And we're here with an hour to spare."

"Now they'll probably be late."

Handing her keys over to the attendant, she slammed her door shut. "Why do you say that?"

"Murphy's law. If we'd been running late, they would have been early, but because we're running early, they'll be late." He stepped aside to follow her down the street. "Trust me. I'm a lawyer. I know all the laws."

"Oh. I bet you do."

"Don't you believe me?" He shot her that cute lopsided grin that highlighted his sense of humor.

"Absolutely." There was no stopping her from grinning back. The morning had flown by and for the first time ever she looked forward, not just to arriving at the lake, but to the journey too.

Her cell phone sounded just as they reached the door to her building. "Hello?"

"Ms. Colby?"

"Yes."

"Your driver is running ahead of schedule. He should be there shortly."

"Okay. Thank you." The rumbling sound of a large truck filled the narrow city street and came to a stop in front of her building. A man hopped out wearing a uniform with an embroidered pocket with the company delivery company logo.

"Looks like the delivery is here a little early." She turned to face him and smiled. "So much for Mr. Murphy."

"Yes indeed," he laughed.

To any observer it would be obvious that the delivery company took extreme care in their task. Not only did they maneuver the large crate inside the tiny elevator and into her apartment without issue, they carefully opened the container for inspection without being asked. The appropriate papers were signed. The delivery team replaced, re-packaged and sealed the crate and handed Zinnia two pages to sign. All in all, they were very well paid and it showed.

"So." David stood by the crate and tapped the top. "Pick up isn't for another four hours and I'm starving. What do you say we do lunch and play tourist?"

Now wasn't that an interesting idea. Born and raised in upstate New York, the only time she'd played tourist growing up was when friends or family came to visit. As an adult living in the city, time was limited. "Tourist sounds fun. What do you suggest?"

"Let's start with the lobster boat over on the west side. I've got a hankering for Katie's lobster roll and this is the best substitute I can think of."

"Oh. I've heard about that." The old ferry boat was converted to a restaurant and ran up and down the Hudson all day long. "They get great reviews from locals and tourists alike."

"Exactly. Grab your keys and let's go."

"Deal." So thrilled with how the day was going, she leaned in and gave him a quick kiss on the cheek and almost tripped over her own feet when she realized what she'd just done. The crazy part was, she wanted to do it again and then some.

● ● ● ●

"You were right. As good as it is, it's not Katie's."

"I don't think there's any place on the planet that can live up to the standard set by Katie and her homemade mayo." Though the sandwich was delicious, David hadn't really expected it to be as good as Katie's.

"And don't forget the fresh made bread." Zinnia popped a last morsel of lobster salad into her mouth.

"Couldn't possibly." From their seats along the rail of the food deck of the former ferry boat, the views of the New York skyline were worth much more than the price of lunch. And like the commercial touted, the company was priceless.

"I can't believe this is the first time I've ever ridden on the Hudson and viewed the skyline for myself."

"It's why locals should play tourist once in a while. Everyone needs to see how the city looks from a vantage point other than the inside looking out."

"Can't argue with you there. But still, there's much to be said for the inside looking out. Central Park, Radio City and the Rockettes, Rockefeller Center, Saint Patrick's Cathedral—"

"Don't forget street vendor hot dogs, warm chestnuts in winter, and a slice of hand-tossed pizza."

Zinnia barked out a laugh. "If you're going to do foods then we have to mention Arthur Avenue."

"That's the Bronx."

"Still New York City."

"True." He collected the used napkins and paper plates and whizzing past a couple strolling hand in hand, wadded them in a bundle and did a perfect rim circle before sinking into the large trash can. "There's also Chinatown."

"Which used to be Little Italy."

"Okay now I'm craving lasagna."

"But you just ate?"

"Since when does that matter?"

"Men," she teased. "Always thinking with their stomachs."

"Come on." He grabbed her hand and tugged her to follow. "Let's watch the boat dock from the upper deck. We've got a couple of hours to kill. We can take a little walk and then decide where to have dinner once the crate is on its way and before heading back to the lake."

"Well, since we mentioned Italian…" she let her words hang.

"A woman after my own heart." He might be teasing but he meant it more than he should. To his delight, they reached the upper deck and her hand was still tightly entwined with his. They found an empty spot to lean against the rail and even though he had no reason to continue holding her hand, he didn't want to let go, and she didn't seem to be at all uneasy about it. The day was looking even brighter.

"There's the pier." She pointed with her free hand. "Guess we beat the crowd. Look at the size of that line."

Another reason for him to be grateful to the fates. Maneuvering off the boat through the disembarking crowd and throng of people waiting to board gave him one more excuse to hang on to her hand. Casually walking cross town, her hand still in his, he felt like a kid in high school out on his first date. Before he realized how long they'd been strolling, neither inclined to let go of the other's hand, they'd reached Fifth Avenue. "Decision time."

Her smile firmly in place, she rolled her eyes skyward. "Are you really hungry already?"

Shaking his head, he chuckled softly. "No. Well, always yes, but that's not what I meant. To our left is Rockefeller Center, to the right the Empire State Building. Which way do we go?"

Turning her head left than right, she bit down, nibbling on one corner of her lower lip. "Uh…"

Her head shifted once again from side to side, her lips puckered full and sweet and he had no idea what she was thinking but if she didn't stop looking so adorable he was going to kiss those lips in front of God and all the passersby.

"I haven't been to the Empire State Building since I was in elementary school. Do you think there's time?"

He had no idea if today would be a day when the lines moved quickly or when half the country had the same idea, but he was willing to try. "Only one way to find out." Tugging on her hand slightly, they turned right and headed down the avenue.

A few blocks down the street Zinnia came to a stop, her mouth dropped open and a wide smile highlighted a twinkle in her eyes. "Kat."

The two women hugged and practically squealed.

"Life in the city looks good on you." Kat eased back, looked her over from head to toe and then squeezed her again. "It's been too long. How did we let all these months go by without making even a little time for a cup of coffee?"

Zinnia shrugged. "I was just thinking the same thing. Only I think it's closer to a year."

"Oh, hell!" Kat moved in for yet another hug.

Shoving his hands in his pocket, David did his best not to resent the woman for breaking the simple physical connection between him and Zinnia.

"David, this is one of my dearest friends, Kathleen Regatta."

The name rang a bell. "From the *Tribune*?"

The woman beamed. "The one and only."

"I read your piece on the veiled extortion in the northeastern refuse industry. Well done."

"Thank you." She beamed like a kid who had been told by Santa that she'd made the Nice List. "Listen. I really want to hang out over a bottle of wine and catch up, but I have an appointment in," she looked at her phone and frowned, "five minutes."

"Go." Zinnia waved her friend up the street. "We'll talk later."

"Promise?"

Zinnia nodded. Kat gave her friend another tight squeeze and hurrying away, quickly disappeared from view.

"She's good." Wanting to hold her hand again, but unsure of the appropriate next move like that awkward teen on a first date, he settled for setting his hand at the small of her back and urging her forward.

"Always has been." Pride easily clung to her words. "For a while there she was torn between journalism and teaching math. What a waste of talent it would have been if she'd stuck with teaching."

David held the door open to the famous and for a brief moment in history, tallest building in the city. In no time they were riding up the multiple required elevators and stepping out onto the main floor. A quick perusal of the souvenir areas and then they proceeded to the outdoor viewing balcony.

"Amazing, isn't it?" Once again, he let his hand come to rest at the small of her back. For a split second he thought he'd felt her lean into his touch.

"Looks even better now that I'm grown up. Doesn't hurt any that I'm tall enough to see over the wall without any help from a tired parent."

Taking advantage of the small area and tourists mulling around them, he tightened his hold on her waist and resisted the urge to thank each person as they hovered nearby.

The moment ended too soon when looking over her shoulder, Zinnia lurched forward, dragging David behind her. "I'd like to find Lady Liberty, if you don't mind." She hadn't waited for an answer, simply took his hand and pulled him along.

"Whatever milady wants." Along with his best grin, he added a playful attempt at a royal bow. Her gaze grew sharp and her smile stronger. Mission accomplished.

Halfway around the large viewing area, she came to a halt and just stared into the distance at the green speck standing proudly in the harbor. "Lady, one of the General's dogs, is named after the Statue of liberty."

He nodded, more interested in the view of her than the famed statue. At this hour the summer sun shone down brightly on her hair. She looked so damn beautiful. Almost angelic. The wind was just strong enough to blow her blonde locks away from her face. A beautiful face. Arm extended, she spun around and almost bumped into him. Whatever protocol might be for working with a beautiful woman was about to get thrown out the door. His hand rose and curled behind her neck, tugged her closer against him, and he stared just a moment into the big blue eyes, waiting for any sign that he was about to get his face slapped.

In the next seconds if anyone asked, he didn't have a flicker of an idea of who moved first, but she was in his arms and his mouth had found hers. Pressed together so tightly that not a single sheet of paper could slip between them, David didn't have the care who was near or watching. Propriety was a far and distant concept, and nothing felt sweeter than Zinnia Colby kissing him back.

CHAPTER TWELVE

Now Zinnia understood why so many romantic movies had their best scenes at the top of the Empire State Building. Maybe it was thinner air. Maybe David really was the best kisser ever. Or maybe she was simply losing her mind. Like the stars of those old-fashioned films, a simple touching of lips, the gentle beat of his heart against hers, and she could swear she heard fireworks bursting and music playing.

"Excuse me," a distant voice drifted past her. A beat later something brushed against her arm.

She didn't know if the low moan that slipped from her throat was because of the kiss or the growing crowd. She was, however, positive this was most definitely no place to explore kissing David Ingram.

Someone bumped into them and she lost her footing. Tightening his hold around her waist, he helped her regain her balance and slowly eased back and sighed. "Not the place for this."

"I was just thinking the same thing." At least she was once her brain was able to put together a cohesive thought.

"We should probably get going." Only he wasn't moving.

Neither was she.

Another voice muttered "excuse me" after bumping into them.

David's hand slid down her side and latched onto hers. "Come on. We don't want to miss the delivery people."

"No. We don't." Words weren't coming easily, but she did agree that atop a popular tourist attraction with a growing crowd was not where she wanted to be.

At the curb, still holding her hand, David raised his arm and waved down a cab. Apparently he was as eager to get back to her place as she was. Whether or not it was for the same reason she had no way of knowing, but she was all for hurrying home.

With the rise in car service, finding a free cab nowadays was pretty easy no matter the time of day. Today was no exception. His arm had barely shot out to wave at an oncoming yellow cab when a big old bubble roofed looking taxi slid to a halt in front of them.

David gave the driver the address and then leaned back into the seat. His arm went from tucked neatly between them, to sliding across her shoulders. "Ever make out in a taxicab?" he teased.

"Nope. Can't say that making out in cabs was something that was ever a thing."

"Always a first time?" He waggled his brows at her.

Her gaze drifted to the cab driver in the front seat busy ignoring them. She was truly tempted. In a matter of minutes something had shifted. Something deep inside had her heart pounding a little harder, her breath coming a little faster, and a giddy zing of excitement rushing up and down her system like she'd never known. If this were any other day in a normal work week, she'd be working hard at her desk and not playing fun loving tourist. Especially not with David.

"Hey." Tucked under her chin, his finger turned her face toward him. "What's wrong?"

"Wrong?"

"You're frowning. Did I misunderstand? If I upset you. If you don't want—"

"No." Her words cut him off and her fingertip stilled his lips. "I guess I was just thinking."

A soft sigh escaped his lips, but relief didn't seem to be the reason. "If that look has anything to do with our kiss, I'm in big trouble."

Look? The frown. He did say she was frowning. And why was she frowning? Lingering in the warm and fuzzy feeling skittering from head to toe, she had to wonder why was she wasn't smiling. Why wasn't she shouting from the highest mountain that in only a few days, David Ingram made her the happiest she'd ever been. If there was such a thing as love at first sight, she'd found it. And that was the root of all her doubts. Was there really such a thing as love at first sight? As an intelligent levelheaded woman who could easily separate fact from fiction, she was pretty sure she was falling head over four inch heels in love with this man. So now all she had to figure out was if that was a good or bad thing—only how the heck was she going to figure that out?

• • • •

David had no idea what was bothering Zinnia. Of course, his not understanding women was nothing new. He knew enough women, and had enough dating experience, and certainly enough education, to readily admit that women were an enigma to be enjoyed, not understood. Or in other words, when it came to Zinnia his computerized brain might have to admit defeat and just go with the flow. Which brought him full circle: why was she frowning?

He brushed a finger across the deep lines between her brows. "That frown is getting deeper. Will it help if I ask the judge and jury to strike the original question from the record?" Because right now he wanted very much to make things right. To replace that crinkled brow with a heartfelt smile.

"Which question?"

"The bit about ever making out in a taxicab."

"Oh, that."

Again, he had no idea why, but the frown slipped from worry to a look more akin to confusion, though the hint of a smile made him feel a tad less concerned he'd completely screwed up.

"Sometimes," she continued, "I have a hard time turning my mind off. I may need to work on just enjoying the moment, stop analyzing so much."

Now he was the one surprised. Analyzing? What was there to analyze? Whatever was running through her thoughts, he wanted nothing more than to remove all negatives and make everything right in her world. He wasn't sure when it started to matter, but seeing her happy suddenly mattered a whole lot to him. More than it should for someone he'd only know a short while.

But wasn't that the rub? He felt as if he'd known her since forever. And didn't that sound like a really bad line from a stupid movie. What was he doing anyway, wanting to make out like a kid in the backseat of a cab? No wonder she'd been frowning. He was behaving like an idiot.

"Now *you're* frowning." She laughed. "What if we start over from the beginning."

"The beginning?"

"Of the conversation," she reassured him with a smile, only to notice the cabbie slowing the car to the curb. They were here. "When we get upstairs."

He shoved a few bills at the cabby and nodded at her. "Deal."

Only that was as far as the conversation got. Just like earlier in the day, the delivery truck pulled up only moments after they did. Hurrying upstairs, she carefully supervised the two moving men loading the crate onto a big dolly and working their way to the service elevator. The packaging inspected, the paperwork signed, and the statue on its merry way, they were ready for the next step.

Standing on the curb as the truck pulled away, he wondered what now? Anxious to get back on even footing, he did his best not to make any more missteps. "Hungry?"

"Actually, yes. Suddenly, I'm starved."

"Still craving Italian?"

"Does pizza count?"

"Absolutely."

"Then I know just the place." She offered him a sweet smile that sent his heartrate galloping. "It's just around the corner."

And just like that, they were strolling down the street holding hands once again.

"What happens now?" He kept looking forward.

"Once we're done with dinner, we should head back to the lake. Might even get there early enough for a tail end of the card games."

He nodded, considering his next words, and opted for sticking with safe. "Do those card games happen every night, all year?"

"Not every night, but most nights, and pretty much all year. There are plenty of repeat tourists who come up and love to join in on occasion and play during warm weather season, but the locals are the ones who keep things going all winter."

"And keep things interesting," he added

"You got that one!" She grinned big and waved an arm at the pizzeria. "Here we are. Johnny's."

Through the large plate glass window someone he assumed was Johnny could be seen standing behind a counter tossing a growing disk of dough up in the air over and over. "I've always wondered how they do that."

"Carefully." She grinned, crossing inside.

The next thing he knew they were seated in a back corner almost playing with the pizza more than eating it. "Johnny is very generous with his cheese."

"Mm." Reaching for another slice, she pulled it toward her, the tip drooping downward, the strings of cheese slowly stretching toward her finally snapping off. "I'm saying five inches. A clear winner so far."

"We'll see." He did the same, easing the piece of pizza toward him, gingerly teasing the gooey cheese into pulling slowly apart. Who knew two people could laugh so hard over strings of mozzarella.

"Ooh, looking go—od," her enthusiasm dropped off as the piece suddenly snapped free in his hands. "Thought it was going to be a record breaker for a second there."

He lifted the floppy tip into his mouth and nodding slowly, mumbled his agreement.

Zinnia did the same, lifting her slice high into the air, her tongue darted out, chasing long strands of dangling cheese. Swallowing hard, he almost choked on his own saliva. The urge to snatch the slice away from her hands and kiss her breathless was suddenly overwhelming. A lot of things were suddenly overwhelming.

He'd loved every second of this very long day. Was looking forward to every second of the long, and what would normally be boring, drive back to the lake. And more surprising than that, when he thought ahead to after her cousin's wedding, and the time when he'd return to his busy life and she to an over demanding job that she loved, a physical pain deep in his gut kicked at him. No matter how he shifted the moving parts, there was little to no chance whatever they had would work away from the carefree summer at the lake world.

The thought and feelings caught him totally off guard. Sitting back a moment, he looked at the woman he'd spent his day with. Spent the last several days with. His new reality smacked him hard on the head. Somehow, in just a short time, he was most definitely, beyond any doubt, falling hard for Miss Zinnia Colby and damned if that didn't make him want to roar. All he had to do was charm the socks off of her so after Heather's wedding Zinnia couldn't picture her life without him.

Content with his new goal, keeping his gaze on Zinnia, he took another bite and his next thought almost brought his heart to a crushing stop. What if he couldn't pull it off?

• • • •

It took all of five minutes walking around the corner for Zinnia to feel as though this routine were a natural part of her life. At her age she'd walked down the street on a date with a man often enough. Yet, something about this felt so totally different. And now, tucked into a booth in the back of Johnny's, she couldn't remember the last time she'd laughed so much over a pizza.

A long time ago when she was a young teen talking to her grandmother, Zinnia had asked her how she could be married to a man who was away for so long and so often. For much of her early childhood on the lake, her grandfather had been deployed and it was Grams who ruled the roost. Zinnia knew it wasn't easy and didn't understand how or why Grams had done it. The answer had been simple, unexpected and at the time made no sense to Zinnia. *He always makes me laugh.*

All of a sudden it made perfect sense. Being able to laugh together over a simple daily moment in life was mountains apart from the storytelling jokester who had people laughing at a party, or the prankster who sometimes made you laugh and sometimes made you spitting mad, or laughing at the unexpected joy of a new experience. A rom-com could make you laugh at the unexpected, but bringing a smile to everyday life was definitely something special. And right about now she could bow down to fate for bringing this man into her life.

"If we get on the road now we should make it back to Hart House by a reasonable hour." A sly grin teased at the corner of David's mouth. "That is, if you let me drive."

Why not? She driven in this morning and frankly wasn't thrilled about dealing with traffic to escape New York City. Besides, letting him drive her car just… felt normal. She dangled her keys in front of him. "Works for me."

Traffic leaving Manhattan wasn't nearly as bad as she had expected. On the ride south, they never bothered to turn the radio on. On the ride north, she discovered middle ground for musical entertainment. Eliminating his liking of classic oldies rock bands like Jethro Tull and Frank Zappa, and discarding her love of classic from her grandparents' era, light jazz or popular top 40 hits post-1980 were wins for the day.

"I wonder if there has ever been any real studies on why the ride home always seems so much faster than the drive going somewhere?" Zinnia propped one foot against the glove box and glanced at the clock.

"I doubt it." He smiled at her. "Looks like we're going to make better time than I thought.

"Eighty miles an hour on the New England Thruway will do that."

David shrugged. "There wasn't much traffic."

"And lucky for you, not many state troopers."

"Wrong time of the month. No one is worried about ticket quotas yet."

Coming around the bend, downtown Lawford could be seen up ahead. Another few minutes and they were turning onto Hart Land.

"Wow. Looks like a full house tonight." From the driveway it was easy for Zinnia to see all the people mulling about or playing cards. The mellow sound of Frank Sinatra crooning "I've Got You Under My Skin" could be heard as soon as they opened the car doors.

"Music is a first for me." David slammed the car door and followed Zinnia up the path.

Zinnia glanced at her wrist. Almost ten thirty. "When the General or Grams turns on the old favorites, that's usually a sign it's going to be a long night. And if they've opened the wine bottles, Louise and Nadine will be in rare form."

"Can't wait." He smiled and came up beside her.

"You sure? It was a long drive after a long day. I'm sure everyone will understand if you want to call it a night."

"Not on your life." Still grinning, he tipped his head toward the house. "This should be a blast."

And that ease with her family and all their crazy friends was just one of the things she loved about him.

"You coming?" He paused at the foot of the porch steps.

Her own thoughts had given her a start, rooting her in place. "Yes. Of course." She shook her head and hurried to catch up, doing her best to take a long look into his twinkling blue eyes. *Loved about him?*

CHAPTER THIRTEEN

"Today has been crazier than a raccoon with rabies." Lucy tied her apron around her waist.

"That doesn't sound good." Zinnia dropped her work bag by her grandmother at the kitchen table.

"George is in bed with some summer cold and you know how men are with a cold," Lucy practically growled. "Your grandmother and I have been scampering up and down to his cabin with juice, and soup, and now he had a craving for Lily's spitzbuben cookies. Good thing I had a frozen batch or I'd have been running into town on top of everything else."

"Everything else?" David poured himself a cup of coffee from the always hot pot on the counter. The one thing he had missed about working up on Eagle's Point today has been the constant flow of hot coffee.

With the lack of indoor plumbing on a beautiful and peaceful mountain top, the last thing Zinnia had wanted was anything to drink, but she had truly enjoyed working high in nature. They both had a long checklist to complete in order to allot the rest of their time at the lake for nothing but vacation. A couple of camp chairs and their laptops, and they had settled in for an afternoon's work. Neither had said much since the objective had been work, and yet the company had added to the surroundings. All in all, another very good day.

Lucy blew a wisp of hair away from her forehead. "The kitchen sink at the Elm cottage sprang a leak."

"Fortunately for us, Lucy knows how to use a wrench." Grams didn't look up from her lump of clay.

Standing at her grandmother's side with a cool glass of water, Zinnia couldn't for the life of her figure out what the lump was supposed to be.

"Where was the General?" David asked. "No, strike that. Today is the afternoon checker game at Floyd's."

It wasn't a question. The litigator's mind had a fascinating way of storing away facts and retrieving them as needed. Zinnia would kill to be able to do that without a spreadsheet in front of her.

"Yoo hoo," an unfamiliar voice carried from the front door.

Lucy turned off the oven light and called out, "In the kitchen."

Just about anyone in town had been to Hart House at one time or other, so it was no surprise to see Mabel's daughter Martha come through the doorway. Well, no surprise that Martha knew where the kitchen was. Why she was here was another story.

Lucy rushed across the kitchen to greet their guest. "I really appreciate you bringing this over. Between George, and the guests, and scrambling to get the roast in the oven on time, I completely forgot we were out of potatoes. There's no way I could have pulled off mashed potatoes on my own tonight."

"No problem. The season is starting to wind down so the diner isn't quite as full and Mom could spare me. I actually appreciated an excuse to get out and enjoy the late setting sun for a change." Martha handed over a bulky paper shopping bag.

"Have you met our guest?" Accepting the handoff, Lucy waved her arm casually at David. "Martha here is a whiz in the kitchen. She and her mother run the local diner."

David looked up from his coffee mug. "How do you do?"

"David's grandfather is a good friend of the General's." The way Lucy bobbed her head in a single gesture of an irrefutable truth, anyone would think she'd declared him the next in line to the British throne, or future president of the United States. Not to mention her suddenly very calm demeanor belied the woman who had just been fussing moments ago. "Can I tempt you to sit for a few minutes? I'm about to pull a blueberry crumble from the oven."

"You know I can't resist your blueberry crumble." Martha's whole face lit up.

"Excellent." Lucy slid an empty plate onto the island and turned to the oven.

Martha looked around the massive island and at David, searching for a place to sit. Except for the stool occupied by David, all the usual options for sitting at the island were not available.

When had all the stools disappeared?

"Oh silly me." Lucy ran off to the back hall and emerged once again with a red wooden stool and of all the sides of the island available, she set it right up next to David.

The way Martha's eyes momentarily widened, it was clear whatever Lucy's plans for today might be, poor Martha had no clue what was about to hit her. The problem, of course, was that neither did anyone else. And that was if, and only if, Lucy was actually up to something. Thinking back over the years, Zinnia could remember multiple times when all hell had pretty much broken loose around the lake, whether with guests, or family, or some inconvenient oddity like the septic system backing up, or an angry raccoon trapped in the pantry, and not once did Zinnia remember Lucy being one iota frazzled or more importantly, botching dinner.

All the *mishaps* over the years, thanks to Lucy's ill-conceived antics, coupled with today's unusually frazzled behavior left Zinnia very leery of the housekeeper's motivation in so much extracurricular chit chat right now just didn't sit right—so to speak.

Lucy proceeded to slip a large slice of her warm crumble onto the plate on the counter and slid it by the empty seat.

"Thanks." Martha hefted her hip up and landed squarely on the seat. Knife in hand, Lucy stared in silence at her visitor, as though waiting for her to do or say something life changing.

"Tell your mom I really do appreciate her bailing me out." Lucy finally turned her back to the woman and carried the mashed potatoes to the warming oven. The woman was definitely up to something or Zinnia wasn't named after a colorful pinwheel flower.

"No problem." About to dive into the warm cobbler, Martha waved Lucy off with a casual and nonchalant move of the hand when panic suddenly filled the young woman's eyes.

Not a half second later, the fork in Martha's hand went sailing across the room. Her other arm flew up in the air as the scene unfolded in very slow motion. On the heels of Martha's scream, seats scratched against the floor as anyone within grabbing distance leapt forward. Closest to her, David let his coffee mug crash to the floor, splattering the hot liquid in every direction as the broken stool shot out from under Martha and he caught her in his arms.

Quickly, missing pieces of the unfolding scene were coming

together in Zinnia's mind. But surely Lucy wouldn't risk breaking an arm or leg of a woman who made her living waiting tables? Not even their scheming matchmaker could have the nerve.

"Are you all right?" The sound of alarm in Lucy's voice had Zinnia double-thinking her first thought.

Still somewhat stunned and practically sprawled across David's lap, Martha nodded.

"Are you absolutely sure?" The way Lucy checked every limb for the tiniest sign of injury had Zinnia scolding herself for thinking ill of Lucy and Martha's broken stool. Risking a broken bone was not on the same level as siphoning gas or locking someone in a shed. Considering the probable outcome, both of those previous mishaps were pretty low risk.

"Everything seems fine." Lucy straightened and waved a finger at Martha, who was still precariously balanced partly on David's lap, but mostly in his arms. "But you should stay still until the paramedics arrive."

And so much for any hopes of innocent Lucy.

"Paramedics!" Martha screeched, instantly springing to her feet and regaining an unsteady balance.

David's arms hovered at either side of the waitress, just in case Lucy was right and she was about to keel over. Poor misguided soul. He had no idea how low Lucy would stoop for a perfect match.

"No paramedics," Martha said a little less frantically. "I am fine. Really, I am."

"I don't know. That was quite a tumble." Lucy stood hands fisted on her hips, head shaking. "Maybe it would be a good idea at least if you went out to the porch and rested a minute with some fresh air. You can have your blueberry crumble while you recover."

Oh boy, was Lucy laying it on thick. Martha had *tumbled* all of a foot into David's waiting arms. It took all of Zinnia's self control not to roll her eyes and sigh like an exasperated teen.

"You don't mind helping her out, do you, David?" Lucy grinned ever so sweetly at her prey.

The guy's eyes rounded wide. What Zinnia couldn't decide was if his response was due to surprise or sudden understanding.

"Of course not," his expression more relaxed, he agreed politely.

"Really," Martha's softer voice took on a more insistent tone, "I'm fine and I really should get back to the diner before Mom starts to wonder what happened to me."

Now it was Lucy who looked suddenly panicked. "Surely you have time to finish one piece of the crumble. It's still warm."

"No. Thank you." She shook her head, raising her hand before Lucy could make another objection. "Next time." The damage had been done. Martha was as spooked as the rest of them.

When was Lucy going to learn?

• • • •

The way Martha hurried out the door, she reminded David of a wild rabbit running from headlights shining on the driveway.

"I do wish she'd sat a bit." Mrs. Hart stared after the empty hall. "I think I'll call Mabel and let her know what happened. Just in case."

"Good idea." Lips pressed tightly together, Lucy nodded and spun on her heel. "I'll call her now."

David took it upon himself to pick up the broken pieces of the stool before somebody tripped over them and really hurt themselves. The bulk of the stool in one hand and the broken leg in the other, he turned to Mrs. Hart. "What would you like me to do with these?"

The well-dressed older woman frowned at the stool. "The back porch will do. We'll take it to the dump in the next trip."

The sound of nails clicking against the wooden floors announced the arrival of the General and his two faithful Golden Retrievers. "In all the years Martha has been awaiting tables at Mabel's, I don't think I've ever seen her move quite that fast. What did you do to her and who did it?"

"Nobody did anything to her," Lucy answered without looking up. "She did take a tumble."

"Yes," Mrs. Hart agreed. "And when he's feeling better we'll need to have George check out these stools and make sure that they're all still secure. Unless you'd like to do it, dear?"

"Why wouldn't the stools be secure?" the General asked. David held up a piece of wood and the General nodded. "Yes. I'll take care of that, but where are the other stools?"

"Here you go." Lucy set two in front of the General and returned to the back porch and reappeared with two more.

David glanced down at the piece of wood in his hand, turned it one-way then the other before looking more closely at the rest of the stool. He had the distinct feeling he had just bumped headlong into what Zinnia had warned him about. Lifting his gaze, he caught Zinnia's attention. Their gazes met and he tipped his head toward the back door. After spending almost all of the last two days together, they seemed to have established a pretty good silent communication system. Without a word, she gave an almost imperceptible nod and crossed the kitchen. As he'd hoped, she knew exactly what he wanted.

The back door slammed shut behind her. "What's up?"

"This." He held out the broken leg from the stool. "I may be a lowly lawyer, but I recognize when a piece of wood has a clean-cut."

"Clean-cut?"

He nodded. "This chair didn't happen to break. The leg was sawed just far enough that it would give away fairly quickly to the weight of a human being."

"Good grief."

"Do you think Lucy could have done this?"

Zinnia shot him a you-have-to-be-kidding look. "Though I admit I don't know what she was thinking. If you didn't have fast reflexes, and Martha hadn't landed on your lap…" Her words trailed off, and she shook her head. "I guess that was the plan all along. To have Martha land in your lap."

"Lucy did seem keen on my going out to the porch with Martha." Though he wasn't terribly sure what could be gained from that.

"What can I say? She's a romantic at heart. Two members of the opposite sex relaxing on the porch under a starry summer night."

"Sounds like an old fifties movie. Starry Summer Night." If not for the absurdity of the entire idea, and the potential danger, David would've found the old broad's efforts amusing. "Should I mention this to the General?"

Zinnia blew out a long deep breath. "I suppose we should. Let me have the leg. I'll tell him when the timing is right."

"Sounds good. Let me know if you want company when you tell him."

"Covering my six?" Her lips curled upward in a cute smile.

"What can I say? Some things about the Marine Corps are simply inherited." He took his time soaking in the woman and the wooden leg she held in her hand. He didn't have to have served time in the Marine Corps to know he would gladly have her back from now on.

"I guess we better get back inside before they think you've started hand carving a new stool."

He let his hand drop to the small of her back. "We wouldn't want them thinking that."

No sooner had he followed her in the kitchen than Poppy came through the doorway, huffing with excitement. "Did you hear the news?"

"What news?" Lucy asked.

"I'm telling you, you'll never believe." The woman was practically bouncing in her shoes. "It's the most exciting thing to happen on this mountain since, well, since forever."

"Don't keep us in suspense, child," Grams said sweetly.

Poppy curled her foot around the leg of one of the stools and three people practically pounced on her, screaming *no*!

"Sit here." The General pulled out one of the kitchen chairs and continued his quiet inspection and testing of the stools.

"Thanks, General."

"Here." Lucy handed her a glass of water. "Drink that before you have a seizure."

Poppy took a long, slow swallow, set the glass on the countertop and spun around to face her audience impatiently waiting. "The FBI has raided that big house up the mountain."

"You're kidding?" several voices said.

"Really?" Grams paused mid-press on her clay.

The pretty redhead drew an X across her chest and held her hand up palm out. "Really. Cross my heart, spit in your eye, honest-to-goodness."

"Why in heaven's name would the FBI care about summer tourists?" Lucy asked.

"Apparently," Poppy straightened her shoulders. "if your houseguest is Carlo Gambini, the FBI cares."

"Who is Carlo Gambini?" Callie asked.

Carlo Gambini. Recognition dawned and David snapped his fingers. "That's it."

"What's it?" Zinnia frowned at him.

"The face I couldn't put my finger on. The man you saw at the flower shop the other day is Carlo Gambini, the one and only."

CHAPTER FOURTEEN

"Carlo Gambini. No way." Zinnia didn't stop shaking her head.

"Yes. Way." David nodded. "The man's been avoiding FBI investigations for years. He's almost as famous for his slipperiness as he is for being the head of one of the largest New York crime families.

"I was reading about that this morning." The General replaced the last of the stools, clearly satisfied with their stability. "Your friend did a great job."

"Your friend?" David's eyes widened in her direction.

"Yes. Kat Regatta. The one we ran into in the city. The General mentioned the other morning she was doing a piece on the Gambinis. But the man from the flower shop is not Carlo Gambini. He's my boss's brother, Charlie."

Eyes still wide, David sat back on his stool.

"Isn't Charlie an Americanization of the Italian Carlo?" Lucy asked.

"Kat's whole piece has been quite interesting. I honestly didn't know much of the family history. It's been rather fascinating. For instance," the General added, "Carlo Gambini's father was briefly married in his youth to one of Connecticut's upper crust families."

"What?" Zinnia took a seat. She wasn't feeling so good all of a sudden.

"Apparently, Gambini senior was intent on building the legit side of the family business. Met a nice girl on vacation, fell in love and they eloped to Vegas. Within weeks, Gambini senior's father was killed in a mob hit and he had to step up and take over. The new Mrs. Gambini was horrified. The marriage was annulled and she went on to marry someone in her respected social circle. The original indiscretion was never publicized and easily forgotten."

Eyes now closed, David pinched the bridge of his nose.

Grams nodded. "That was the beauty of the days before internet, cell phone photography, and social media news alerts. Hiding a mistake like that would have been easier. Especially then. Money always talks. It used to be that old adage 'not what you know but who you know' was very easily achieved if you had money. Nowadays every nosy neighbor and newsman comes out of the woodwork searching for dirt on other people. Even here."

"I just think it's crazy that we have had the FBI lurking in town and no one knew it." Poppy was still nearly giddy with excitement.

The General shrugged. "According to the news, there have been a lot of arrests in the past few days. Guys with names like Princie—the crowned prince of the family, Lenny the Goat—"

"What an awful name. I mean, I know if he's a mobster he has to be a bad guy, but at least give him a better animal, like a horse or a tiger," Poppy suggested.

"Apparently he's a bit sloppy. Someone once said his place looked like the inside of a goat's stomach."

"And the guy's still around to tell the story?" Callie's question dripped with sarcasm.

"Doubtful." The General shrugged.

A cell phone sounded and everyone glanced at Zinnia's computer bag.

"Of all times for the reception to be good." Zinnia grabbed the thing from her bag and seeing her boss's number, sucked in a deep breath. "I'll take this in the other room."

She took a few steps toward the hall and finger to her ear, answered. "Hello?"

"Where the hell have you been?" Her boss didn't sound happy at all.

"My family's lake house." He knows that. "Is something wrong?"

"You know damn well something is wrong. How could you?"

Her mind started scrambling for what could make him so angry. The only thing that popped into mind was yesterday's shipping efforts. "Did they lose the statue? Break it? It was completely intact when they checked the crate before hauling it off."

"Statue? What are you talking about?"

"The one purchased a few weeks ago from that online auction. It was delivered to my apartment by mistake and I was able to have it turned around the same day and sent to your house in Connecticut as originally planned."

"I don't give a rat's tail about that."

Considering the thing cost him five figures, that wasn't the reply she'd expected.

"You signed an NDA."

"Yes." Of course she'd signed a non-disclosure agreement. She wasn't following the thread of this conversation very well.

"You're not allowed to discuss anything that pertains to me or my family with anyone for any reason at any time. Ever."

"I understand that. And I've respected it. My family doesn't even know I work for you."

"One damn woman connects the dots and years of patiently planning, building, down the crapper with a single flush. How much did she pay you?"

"What?"

"Never mind. It doesn't matter." She could almost see him pacing as he spoke, gathering his thoughts. "I've been advised to terminate your contract immediately. You'll receive notification via certified letter."

The call disconnected and Zinnia was left staring at the phone. What the heck had just happened?

• • • •

This couldn't be happening. What were the odds that the socialite ex of a Gambini exposed in a news story and his disgruntled client's socialite mother with a secret past were one and the same? That David would be unknowingly advising said client against Zinnia? There were eight and half million people living in New York City. The odds of her being the admin in question had to be humongous, colossal, astronomical.

"They say truth is stranger than fiction." Mrs. Hart tinkered with a small blob on the bigger blob of clay.

"It gets even stranger." The General scratched behind Lady's ear.

"It seems the Connecticut socialite married her high school sweetheart very quickly after the annulment from Gambini. As would be expected of the social elite, wedding invitations were sent six weeks in advance according to protocol. Due to the young couple's history, no one questioned the lack of a formal engagement party and a fairly quick wedding. Nor was the birth of a honeymoon baby questioned either. Although, according to Kat's story in the *Tribune*, the honeymoon baby wasn't born a scant eight months later, a perfectly acceptable happening for a first born son, but six months after the big wedding. Infants vary in size so much that after a few months it's much easier to explain a big boy. By childhood, a few months make no difference at all."

"So what you're saying is there's a socialite Gambini running around Connecticut?" Lucy pulled out a couple of handfuls of silverware and handed them over to Callie and Poppy. "Would you guys set the table, please? Dinner is almost ready and the rest of the crew should be here shortly."

The two nodded, each grabbing a stack of plates as well.

"That's exactly what I'm saying. It's hitting all the papers and tabloids now." The General shook his head. "You'd think the world would have more important things to deal with than some socialite's offspring and his political aspirations."

"Not if you consider the two men sniffing around here today." Mrs. Hart stared at her project with one eye open. David doubted that would help.

"What men?" The crease between the General's brows deepened.

Taking small halted steps, Zinnia walked back into the kitchen, her gaze on her phone. Slowly lifting her head, her eyes leveled with David's. "I've been fired."

"What?" Poppy jumped to her feet and hurried to her cousin's side.

David's stomach did a backflip. Those odds were rapidly dwindling.

"What on earth for?" the General groused, his earlier question to his wife forgotten.

"I wish I knew." Zinnia dropped her gaze to the phone and then raised it to her grandfather. "That was the most confusing conversation I have ever had. But apparently, somehow he thinks I broke our nondisclosure agreement."

And that was the stone that sank David's already upset stomach to the floor. So much for astronomical odds. His client and her boss were one and the same and Carlo Gambini was smack dab in the middle of everything. And as soon as everyone in this room figured out his connection, he would become persona very non grata.

At the chiming of the doorbell, Poppy hollered from the hall, "I'll get it."

"Now who would be ringing the bell?" the General asked.

Gram's looked up from her questionable work of art. The first time David had ever seen her scowl.

The conversation came to a halt as all curious eyes remained on the doorway.

"Evening, everyone." A large man in uniform nodded respectfully at the head of the Hart household. "General."

"Evening, Sheriff."

The imposing man removed his sunglasses and slipped them into his breast pocket. Sucking in deep breath, he blew out what sounded like a reluctant sigh. "I have something for you, Miss Colby."

All eyes followed the folded paper as he handed it off to Zinnia.

"Sorry about this." With a nod of his head, he turned on his heel, wished the General good evening again, and let himself out of the house.

"Dare we ask?" Callie came up beside her cousin.

Quickly scanning the pages, the color drained from Zinnia's face. Eyes closed, she lifted her gaze away from the papers in her hands and blew out a sigh as deep as the remorseful sheriff. "I'm being sued."

* * * * *

Sam was suing her for breach of contract. Her gaze lifted to David. "Looks like I might need a lawyer."

"Yeah. About that." He cleared his throat and glanced around the room.

"Sued?" The General snatched the paper from her hands. "What exactly is this all about?"

"I told you, I don't know." Zinnia squeezed her eyes shut and then snapped them open as if expecting the situation to have changed.

David cleared his throat again. "It may have something to do with your boss's brother and your friend's expose."

"Charlie? What does he have to do with my getting fired?"

"Zinnia." He took a step toward her, then looking around the room, eased back onto the stool. "Charlie is without a doubt Carlo Gambini so if Charlie is his brother then he's Carlo Gambini's brother."

"Which means," Poppy went wide eyed, "you *are* working for the mob."

"I am not." Zinnia actually stomped her feet like a petulant toddler. "Sam Emerson is a respectable citizen." A nice guy. A family man. None of this fit. None of it.

"Samuel Emerson?" The General flipped back to the front page of the papers she'd been served with. "Sweetie, it looks like David is right."

Rarely did the General ever call any of his grandchildren by anything other than their given names. When a term of endearment came out, that usually meant something big was about to happen. Like the time he called Poppy Buttercup just before informing her she needed to go to the hospital to have her tonsils out.

"Samuel Emerson is the socialite's son. The one who in reality is a Gambini. He and Carlo are half brothers."

"What are you talking about?" None of this was making any sense. Not her boss, not her grandfather, not David. Had the whole world gone mad?

Handing her back the papers, her grandfather walked over to the recycling bin in the kitchen and retrieved a newspaper. "Here. Page five. That will explain it all."

As quickly as she could, she perused the piece her friend had written. Any other time or circumstance and she might have enjoyed reading the story. When she came to the part about socialite elopement, annulment, and then immediate marriage to her high school sweetheart, the pieces started to fall into place. "So Charlie *really* is Carlo."

All the heads in the room nodded.

"I think I need a drink." She sank into the nearest kitchen chair. "That's why Sam acted so weird."

"Weird how?" David asked.

"I don't usually work at the main headquarters, but there was a lot going on this one time and he couldn't be in two places at once so I went to work in his office. Charlie startled me when he suddenly appeared in the room. First, I wasn't sure how he got past the iron man assistant guarding the door like a Marine, but when Charlie explained he was Sam's brother, it made sense. That is until Sam came into the office, saw Charlie, and like a cartoon, I could see the red rising up his neck flushing his cheeks. There were some muffled words through clenched teeth about knowing he wasn't allowed there. About knowing never to come. But I thought it had just been some sibling or family squabble of some kind and knowing how intense my boss could be, I figured he was holding a grudge." She lifted the newspaper, the black ink a blur. Not in her wildest dreams could she have thought up something like this.

"Does your boss know you and Kat were childhood best friends?" Callie asked.

Abandoning their master, Lady and Sarge came to sit at her feet. Lady gently rested her head on Zinnia's lap. Zinnia scratched the dog's ear and nodded at her cousin. "She was one of three character references I used."

"From the looks of it," the General moved beside her and rested his hand on her shoulder, "I'd say you're the victim of circumstantial evidence."

"The question is, how long is it going to take and how much will it cost me to prove that?"

Across the room David shifted uncomfortably on the stool, but didn't say anything. No one in the room said a word. Not even Lucy, who rarely was at a loss for something to say, no matter how inappropriate.

"If you'll excuse me a minute." David pushed to his feet and ignoring all the eyes in the room on him, took a few steps closer to Zinnia. "I have to make a very important phone call. After that, we need to talk."

Before Zinnia could respond, her sister Iris practically burst into the room. Her gaze narrowed in on Zinnia. "You'll never guess who I ran into on the porch."

"Our porch?" The General looked over her shoulder.

Iris nodded, crossing the kitchen, her steps purposeful, her expression stony. "They're looking for Zinnia."

"Who is?" The General moved closer to the doorway and casually glanced into the hall.

"The FBI," she said over her shoulder to her grandfather, then leaning into her sister, she softly whispered, "What have you done?"

"Nothing. I swear."

"Then why—"

"Excuse us." Two men in suits, in Lawford, in the dead heat of summer, stood at the doorway. "We'd like to speak to Zinnia Colby."

Grams stepped back from her project and smiled. "Gentlemen, you're back."

CHAPTER FIFTEEN

"They're back?" Standing up, Zinnia looked to her grandmother. "What do you mean *back*?"

Mrs. Hart smiled. "These nice gentlemen were here earlier asking for you. I mentioned you were out of reach."

Dressed in flowing white pants with a tie die silk top, Mrs. Hart looked the epitome of an aged hippy. The woman also had more class in her little pinky than any woman David had ever met. Her mild manner combined with her demure nature might lead most people to confuse her casual responses for someone a bit addled, but if there was one thing David was sure of, it was that this woman was sharp as a tack. Sharper.

"They were asking all sorts of questions." Fiona Hart smiled at the men. Not the sincere grin that always made a stranger feel at home, but one that said they might have ticked her off, but she would remain gracious.

Reading her eyes like he might a juror, David was pretty sure they had indeed done just that earlier today.

"I explained to these nice gentlemen…" She turned to face them. "Where did you say you were from?"

The one man almost blushed as the other mumbled, "We didn't. FBI, ma'am."

"Yes. I thought as much." She returned her attention to her granddaughter. "I explained that we know very little about our new neighbors across the hill, but I'm sure now that you and," she paused and turned to face him, "David are back, the two of you would be more than happy to answer any of their questions."

And there was the set up. He almost smiled, imagining the wild goose chase of a conversation she must've set the two agents on earlier today. She wanted David to be here if they returned. While his specialty might not be criminal law, he still remembered more than enough from law school to keep Zinnia from accidentally falling into the FBI's trap.

"We'd like to speak to you alone, please." The taller man with graying temples spoke first.

"Is there somewhere quiet we could go?" the second man asked. Both stone-faced. Though David would be too if he had to wear a suit in this heat.

The General stepped forward and extended his hand. "Allow me to introduce myself. I'm General Harold Hart, United States Marine Corps, retired. I'm sure whatever the nature of the questions you may have, there's no reason the family cannot remain." He turned to face David. "Is there, David?"

"The General does have a point, gentlemen." It might not be a good one in the FBI's opinion, but he could play poker as well as the next guy.

"And you are?" the tall one asked.

"David Ingram. Attorney at law." Intent on the two FBI agents, he hadn't noticed Poppy and Callie take seats on the stools directly behind Zinnia. Even Lucy and Mrs. Hart had moved to stand at either side of the two granddaughters. The wall of family support was impressive. If he ever got in serious trouble, he certainly wouldn't mind having this family on his six.

The two men quickly surveyed the situation. David could almost see the wheels of their minds turning as they weighed their options and considered how much trouble was the interview worth. He was almost positive he recognized the moment when they decided not to lock horns with a Marine Corps general, an attorney, and how ever high up the proverbial ladder their connections might go. Although, the way the men surveyed the wall of determined females, David suspected the granite faced women may have been the deciding factor.

For the next twenty minutes the two men peppered Zinnia with questions about any interactions between her boss and men like Princie, Lenny the goat, Salvatore Castellano, and of course, Carlo Gambini himself.

As David expected, Zinnia was unfamiliar with the cast of characters, and continued to refer to Carlo as Charlie. The same questions and the same answers volleyed back and forth until restlessness grew thick in the room.

The taller man closed a notebook and slipped it into his breast pocket. "This will do for now. Someone will get back with you if we have any more questions."

If the tick in the back of the General's jaw was any sign, the four star would see to it that there were no more questions.

Her polite smile intact, Mrs. Hart escorted the two men out of the room and out of their home. Without the need for words, her body language clearly informed the men that they were no longer welcome.

"This is surreal." Zinnia plopped down on a nearby kitchen chair. "How was I supposed to know the guy was a mobster?"

Poppy shrugged. "If it makes you feel any better, I didn't know what he looked like until Kat's story."

"Carlo has been the brunt of many a TV special. He's been harder to nab than Al Capone." Iris shrugged at her sister.

"Not this time." Callie came to give her cousin a supportive hug. "The news reports are throwing around words like racketeering and wire fraud."

David waited for Callie to step back before casually approaching Zinnia. Unsure how much of their upgraded relationship she wanted to share with her family, he squatted in front of her and ignored the banter and gazes. "You okay?"

She nodded. "No wonder Sam was so angry at me."

"Accusations of criminal activity tends to make people pretty edgy." He dared reach for her hand and squeezed.

"I suppose." She sighed and then straightened her shoulder. "But how could he think I would sell him out like that?"

The fire in her eyes made him feel just a tad better. Pushing up on his feet, he stood at his full height. He should have known better than to worry about her. She and all her family would have ruled the Amazons. But he still needed to deal with a few things or he might be the next one on the hot seat. "I have to make a call. I'll be back shortly."

She nodded.

"General," he turned on his heel to face the man still red faced with irritation, "if I need it, may I use the landline?"

"In my office."

"Thank you." By now David knew his way around the ground

floor of the Hart house as well as the family. Heck, in such a short time he already felt as though he were family.

Closing the door behind him, he took in the view from the General's desk. Not a bad way to do business. Even if the man was retired. He pulled out his phone and scrolled for the correct number. Phone ringing in his ear, he noticed his grandparents in a nearby photo. Ten couples all dressed to the nines, the photo must have been taken at some official event.

"Hello?"

Hearing the increased aggravation in his client's tone, David returned the photograph to its spot on the desk. "Sam."

"This is insane! My phone hasn't stopped ringing. My private phone. Whatever happened to the right to privacy!" Sam could have probably been heard all the way at the lake without assistance from a telephone.

"We live in an open book world. You knew this could happen."

"I could also get hit by a bus but what are those odds?"

David knew darn well there was no point in answering that question. "Things aren't always what they seem."

"What they seem?" For the next several minutes, Sam went on ranting over unappreciative employees and bloodthirsty news reporters always searching for a story no matter what it cost anyone. By the time the man had stopped his tirade, David had failed to get in even a word or two.

"Sam. Listen to me. I think you need to take a step back."

"Why the hell would I want to do that!"

"Because it's why you pay me the big bucks."

"And that's why I moved forward. My attorneys implemented every one of your suggested changes to our boilerplate NDA. You assured me I'd have an iron-clad contract and could hang whoever breached it out to dry."

Sucking in a deep breath, he blew it out fast and hard. "First of all, hanging anyone out to dry is not going to put the cat back in the bag."

"I have my people working on damage control now. Damn that woman."

"And that's why you have to take a step back before you find yourself in a counter lawsuit for slander, wrongful termination, and slapped with punitive damages."

"What the hell are you talking about? I have an iron-clad contract and that blabbermouth broke it."

"That's slander."

"Not if it's true."

"And you know this how? Remember, I very clearly laid out that all breaches of contract needed to be carefully documented."

"And I did."

That made the knot in his stomach twist. Under normal circumstances, Sam was a very careful businessman. "Okay. What do you have?"

"Along with the reporter's name as a personal reference on Zinnia's application, I have additional school records showing the friendship dates back to high school."

"And?"

"What do you mean and?"

The pressure on his lungs eased. "You have telephone records of recent conversations? Restaurant bills from a meeting. Photographs are better?"

"Well. No."

"No?"

"You're telling me you expect to win in court with guilt by association without proof of association, or did the reporter name her sources and your assistant is on that list?" He knew perfectly well that wasn't the case.

"No reporter worth her salt gives up her sources."

"So you have other proof that will hold up in a court of law?"

Sam hesitated a beat. "I'll get it. She's guilty."

"Okay. Now let's say I can provide irrefutable eyewitness testimony that until yesterday, after all the leaks came to light, these two school friends have not seen each other or spoken in months?"

"That's not possible."

"This isn't conjecture. I'm telling you, I know firsthand of an eyewitness to a conversation that shows these women have not seen each other or spoken since long before this article was a twinkle in the reporter's eye. Now you tell me, are you that sure you can find the proof you'll need to win your case in a court of law?"

• • • •

"Everything will work out." Arm around Zinnia, Grams leaned against her. "No matter how bleak things look on the surface, when you're in the right, life has a way of bringing things together in the end."

"I know." Zinnia let her head rest on her grandmother's shoulder. The woman had always been a ray of perpetual sunshine. The optimist in the family. But this blow was tough. "A lawsuit is going to make a reference unlikely."

"I hope that phone call with David isn't going to take too much longer." Lucy doused the roast in its own juice and closed the oven door. "I can only delay this roast for so long."

"I'm not really very hungry."

"Not even for some of my sweet cornbread?"

Zinnia smiled. "Well. Maybe one—or two."

"Atta girl."

The front door slammed shut. First Jake appeared in the doorway, followed close behind by Lily's husband Cole.

"Is it true?" Jake asked.

"That depends on what." Grams eased away from Zinnia.

Lily's husband Cole came to a stop next to the General. "The FBI is—"

Ralph stormed into the kitchen. "Whatever they want, don't say a word. We'll get you a good lawyer. The best."

The back door swung open. Nadine practically leapfrogged over Louise, waving her pointy finger at Zinnia. "I'm in law enforcement, honey. You have the right to remain silent. You have the right to an attorney and we will see to it you get the best lawyer in the country."

"That's what I said!" Ralph snapped.

"They're right." Louise pushed her way in front of Nadine. "I have savings. I don't need to cruise the Greek Islands. Besides, only old people take those cruises."

Old people? Coming from Louise, the statement almost had Zinnia laughing out loud.

"No one get their knickers in a wad." Suddenly in the hall doorway, Thelma waved her arms at everyone. "I have a cousin who is an assistant to the neighbor of a Senator's aide. We'll get this whole mess taken care of in no time."

Zinnia looked around the room, the hum of friends and family snapping questions and answers at each other growing louder. "Thank you everyone, but I think—"

"So it's true." Floyd appeared out of nowhere. "I thought Betty had lost her mind, but when Mabel said she'd served coffee to two men in suits asking all sorts of questions about Zinnia, Hart House and the latest guest at the big house." He whistled. "I just knew it was trouble."

"Mabel?" Zinnia said at the same time Lucy muttered, "Betty?" and the decibel of chatter in the room jumped a notch.

A sharp whistle pierced the air. With her pinky fingers still poking into her mouth, Katie O'Leary stood glaring at all the people no longer talking at once. "Who here has the facts, only the facts, and nothing but the facts?"

"That would be me." Hand in the air, fingers waving, David walked into the kitchen and stopped beside Zinnia. "And just in case anyone has forgotten, *I'm* a very good lawyer."

"Thank you." Zinnia was hoping she could count on his help.

His gaze softened and he sighed. Leaning closer, he quietly whispered, "We'll see what you have to say after I speak my piece."

All sorts of unpleasant thoughts suddenly scrambled to the forefront of her mind. From she was in bigger trouble than she thought, to under the circumstances with the FBI he wasn't going to be able to associate with her anymore. The latter scared the heck out of her much more than any amount of trouble.

"There isn't any trouble for anyone." David straightened and faced all the friends in the room. "I've had the chance to speak with Mr. Emerson and am pleased to report he has seen the error of his judgment and will be withdrawing all legal actions."

"Really?" Bolstered with excitement, she sprang from the seat and threw her arms around him and kissed him hard on the lips. Wondering how he knew Sam took a few long seconds to come to mind. "Why?"

"Let's just say I have an inside line and you have a witness to your innocence."

"I do?"

"Remember in New York when we ran into Kat?"

She nodded.

"You both mentioned not seeing each other for almost a year." She nodded again. Not sure how she felt about all this. About his hand in it. But then she reminded herself of the hollow feeling that took root when she thought he might say they couldn't continue. Whatever was going on, all that mattered was it was behind her and he wasn't leaving. A smile easily teased her lips. Once again, Grams was right.

CHAPTER SIXTEEN

What was it about the fresh lake air that made waking up in the early morning so difficult? Or perhaps it was merely the late night card games that often rolled into the next day. Though this morning he had no excuse. After dinner last night, despite the resolution of Zinnia's lawsuit peril, no one had been of the mind to play cards. Instead, the diminished crowd had gathered in the den, and munching on garlic parmesan popcorn, and spitzbuben cookies for those folks with a sweet tooth, everyone had settled into their favorite chair for an evening marathon of the Andy Griffith show on an oldies TV channel. He and Zinnia had shared the sofa with Heather and Jake.

They'd had little opportunity to discuss the events earlier in the evening. Almost nothing was said of Sam, other than dropped lawsuit or not, there wasn't enough money in the world to make her go back and work for him or his companies. David couldn't argue. He felt the same way, but at least he could feel sure that Sam would no longer try to smear Zinnia's professional name.

"Morning," a now very familiar voice mumbled near him. Very near him. Too near him.

Opening one eye, he could see the sun was barely peeking through the window. The den's windows. He was still on the Hart House sofa, only it wasn't late at night and he wasn't alone.

The last thing he remembered was Zinnia spread out on the sofa, her head on his lap, the friends having gone home, only family was left. Soon it was down to only Zinnia, Poppy, Mrs. Hart and him remaining up to watch more of the marathon. Clearly, he'd faded to dark soon after that.

Still squinting through one eye, he turned his gaze to the opposite end of the sofa. A slight smile on her lips, eyes closed, Zinnia's snuggled into a pillow. Funny, he didn't remember pillows. Following her form, his gaze stopped at the tip of her toes, inches away from his face. Both eyes now wide open, he blinked and taking in another pillow tossed aside, he realized somehow they had gone from curled up watching television on one half of a couch to spread out, side by side, in opposite directions. How the heck had they pulled that off?

Her toes stretched and wiggled like a cat kneading its paws. "How'd you sleep?"

"Considering I'm on about twelve inches of sofa, pretty good. You?"

"Mm," she half mumbled, half moaned, and suddenly being sprawled out together on the family sofa didn't seem like such a good idea.

The aroma of fresh brewing coffee reached him about the same time he heard the clattering of pots and pans in the kitchen. They weren't the only two awake. The clicking of paws coming down the stairs signaled the impending arrival of the General.

Gently patting her leg, he gave her a gentle nudge. "Time to get up. The family is coming down for breakfast."

The response of another moan, and a full body stretch, didn't make slipping out from behind her any easier. With the descending footsteps growing louder, pressing up on his arms and swinging his legs over her like a gymnast on a pommel horse, he managed to find his footing and be upright as the General entered the room. "Morning, sir." The urge to stand at full attention and salute was unusually strong.

Mrs. Hart sidled up by her husband. "Good morning. I hope you weren't terribly uncomfortable on the sofa?"

"No, ma'am." He couldn't bring himself to relax.

Her smile brightened. "Oh, good. You were both out like lights so I did my best to tuck a pillow under your heads, but I see the blanket wasn't necessary."

Following the direction of her gaze, he noticed a large quilt puddle on the floor. "No, ma'am."

One brow rose high on the General's forehead. "You sure you've never been in the military?"

"Yes, sir. I mean, no, sir. I mean—"

"At ease." The General shook his head, chuckled, and turned on his heel. "I think you need coffee."

Mrs. Hart stepped into the room. "Feel free to use the bathroom upstairs if you'd like to freshen up a bit."

"Thank you."

She reached out, ran her fingers gently down his arm and smiled first at him, then at Zinnia, who had now managed to work herself into an upright position, though her gaze was still sleepy. "Thank you. For everything."

"I see everyone's up bright and early." A large platter in her hand, Lucy popped her head into the room. "Thought you might like to know with all the FBI commotion yesterday I forgot to tell you something. Yesterday was my day to give the General's office a good once over. Went to plug in the vacuum and realized that internet thingy was unplugged."

"Internet thingy?" For possibly the first time that he'd seen, Mrs. Hart frowned.

"You know," Lucy scrunched her face, "that box with all the colored lights."

"I think she means the modem," David provided.

"Whatever I mean," Lucy pointed herself toward the dining room, "you should be able to work now."

He gave a short nod, and kept his gaze on the still frowning Mrs. Hart following after her housekeeper. The woman now out of sight, he turned to Zinnia. "Unplugged."

"Yeah." Zinnia shook her head. "Wonder why the General didn't notice that?"

"Mm." So did he, but his rumbling stomach reminded him there was a breakfast worthy of a king in the other room. "I think I may run down to the cabin and take a quick shower. It just doesn't feel right to show up to breakfast in yesterday's clothes."

"Agreed." Zinnia bobbed her head and pushed to her feet. "Meet you in the dining room in twenty."

"Deal." Taking hold of her hand, he leaned forward and placed as gentle a kiss on those beautiful soft lips as he could. Anything more and he feared he'd never make it to the cabin, family house or not.

Full of inexplicable energy for a man who had slept on a cramped sofa, he bounded down the path and was back at the main house in record time.

"Where's the fire?" Heather came down the staircase and met him in the grand hall.

"Just hungry, I guess."

"Right." She smiled and linked elbows with him. "Come on. I have a feeling about you."

"Good or bad?"

Her head tipped back and she barked a laugh. "All good."

In the dining room, the table was nearly full. Poppy, Zinnia, Jake—who stood, grinning at Heather, and patted the chair beside him—Cindy and Alan, as well as Zane and Callie. When grandchildren came along the Harts were going to need a bigger room.

His gaze fell on the empty seat beside Zinnia and he smiled. He liked that the spot beside her was his. He liked that a lot. As usual the breakfast was hot and delicious and worthy of any five star hotel. Lucy might be a little nuts when it came to matchmaking, but she was indeed master of her own kitchen.

Heather's phone sounded.

"Oh, I hope it's not another emergency." Grams looked over the rim of her coffee cup.

"No. It's Lily." Heather swiped the phone. "You're on speaker."

"Where are you?"

"At the house. Why?"

"Why? You were supposed to be here thirty minutes ago."

Heather turned her wrist and looked at her watch. "Oh, crud. Was that today?"

"Yes, that was today. Is today."

"Right. We'll be there in a few."

"Perfect." Lily cut off the call.

"What's today?" Jake asked.

"The cake tasting."

"At this hour of the morning?" Poppy's voice rose a notch.

Heather's chair scraped against the hardwood floor. "For Lily, this is almost the end of the day."

"What I want to know is with the wedding only two weeks away, why are you only *now* tasting cakes?" Zinnia asked.

"Well," Heather linked hands with Jake, "it's not like I have to pick a baker, just a flavor."

Poppy's face crinkled in confusion. "How many flavors are there for wedding cake?"

"You'd be surprised. Actually, *I* was surprised." Heather shrugged and waved a finger around the table. "Who wants to come with us?"

Zinnia looked at him, brows raised.

He shrugged one shoulder. "Why not?" The next thing he knew, two carloads were on their way to the Pastry Stop.

"Okay." Lily sat everyone at the quaint tables in the front of the small bakery. Well, the front eatery was small. From the quick tour he got, the inner workings were pretty darn big. "There are three choices for cake and three choices for frosting."

"I already know I want Italian cream icing." Heather flashed a toothy grin at her cousin.

"I know. But there's a groom's cake to decide also."

"There is?" Jake asked.

Lily's spine snapped straight. "You don't want a groom's cake?"

Facing his fiancée, Jake asked, "Do I?"

Pretty much everyone in the place burst into varying stages of a chuckle.

Lily rolled her eyes. "Never mind. Taste now. Decide later."

The first dish in front of her, Heather stuck her fork into the slice. Sealing her lips around the fork, she closed her eyes and tipped her head back with a soft, low moan. "Definitely this one."

Jake took a bite. "This is great. Have we had this before?"

"No." Lily shook her head. "It's my newest effort. Vanilla almond with a hint of lavender."

"Oh, this is good," some other voices concurred.

"Okay." Heather pushed to her feet. "That's the one."

"Wait." Lily's eyes rounded. "You can't decide on the first one."

"Why not?"

"Because you can't." Lily waved to the other cakes on the counter. "What if you like another flavor better? You haven't tried the vanilla raspberry. That one's very popular for wedding cake."

"I don't have to." Heather smiled up at Jake. "I've tasted a lot of cake in my life. I know when I find a good one."

"When you find the right one you know it. Simple." Jake's fingers linked with his fiancée's.

"Simple," Heather repeated.

The two looked at each other with enough love to melt the frosting on all the cakes. If David hadn't seen it with his own eyes he wouldn't believe it. That sort of sappy was only in movies. Or so he thought.

• • • •

"I can't believe she made up her mind after only one cake." Poppy collapsed in the big easy chair that flanked the leather sofa.

Callie flopped into another nearby chair. "What gets me is she didn't want to stay to test the rest of the cakes. I mean, when do you have an excuse to eat that much of Lily's baking?"

"Right!" Poppy grinned.

"Absolutely." Zinnia did steal a few bites of the vanilla raspberry. It was better than delicious, but Heather was right. The almond lavender was to die for. That was definitely the one.

"Who's up for some of my fresh lemonade?" Lucy asked from the doorway.

Multiple voices responded, "Me!"

"I'll help." Zinnia took a step toward the kitchen and David grasped her hand and stepped in close.

"Listen, it's early and a beautiful day. What do you say we go for a little walk?"

"Sure. Just let me help Lucy a minute."

He nodded. "I need something from the General's office anyhow. I'll take care of that and meet you in the kitchen."

"Works for me." Pretty much anything David said at this point worked for her. They'd had a bit of a chance, not much, to talk about yesterday and all the crazy business with Sam. An initial flare of anger that David had been a key player on the legal team that almost ruined her career died down when she realized he was only doing what he did best, the same as she had. In the end, what mattered was that he stood up for her against a contract he had helped make ironclad.

"Which cake did she pick?" Lucy pulled a pitcher of lemonade from the fridge.

Zinnia took several tall glasses from the cupboard. "Vanilla lavender almond."

"Oh, that is a good one."

"You've had it?"

Lucy filled the glasses nodded. "She was tinkering with the flavors when she was here last week."

"I swear, if I lived here full time, I'd be big as a house." Pulling out a large wooden tray, Zinnia transferred the drinks and carried them to the other room.

"If things don't work out, you could always be a waitress." Callie retrieved a drink.

"Handling those big trays takes talent," Poppy joined in the tease.

"Hardy har har," Zinnia joked back, but the thought had actually crossed her mind. Not that she believed for a minute it would be necessary. She was good at what she did. Very good. Back in the kitchen, she wiped the tray down and slid it into the cabinet.

David came up behind her, arms around her waist, and let his chin come to rest on her shoulder. "You ready?"

"Sure am. Have any place in mind?"

Fingers linked, they waved at Lucy on their way out the door. "I thought it might be nice to head up to Eagle's Point."

"Even though we don't need the internet?" Her eyes crinkled with teasing laughter.

"Even though," he repeated. His cheeks actually hurt from smiling so hard. "Though we'd only walk the part that's not too tiresome, but has plenty of reward at the top."

"As long as we take the Jeep up the drivable part of the road, or we'll be needing pulmonary resuscitation when we reach the peak."

By the car already, he twirled her into the fold of his arms and kissed the tip of her nose, before opening the door for her with a smile. "That could be arranged."

"Sometimes I wish I didn't have to go back to the city in order to rebuild my customer base and earn a living." She pulled onto the main road.

"I know. At least, I do now. But it would be kind of hard teaching law at Floyd's barbershop."

Zinnia laughed. "That it would. You like what you do?"

"Very much. Sometimes I get inundated grading papers and the trappings of the classroom. Then some kid comes along and reminds me it's not about the job, it's about the kids. Well, I guess at twenty-two or more, I can't really call them kids."

"No, you can't." She slowed for the turn up to Eagle's Point and glanced in his direction. "Got any one kid in particular in mind?"

He nodded. "Had a kid come into my office before I left town. His mom was dealing with cancer. Of course, he was pretty upset. We talked a bit. It's tough manning up for your family when you're barely twenty-three, but this young man did just that. Was there for his sisters and his mother, *and* he took care of school business. Got an A too."

"That's nice to hear." She pulled off the mountain road onto the patch of clear the family used for parking.

"He called this morning as I was heading to the cabin for a quick shower. Wanted me to know his mom had come through surgery with flying colors and the pathology results had come back." He threaded his fingers with hers and taking a step up the mountain, squeezed her hand in his. Tightly. "Stage two."

"Oh, dear."

"No. With the cancer she has that just shot her survival odds up to over 90%."

"Oh, that is good news."

"Yes. Yes, it is."

Holding hands, they slowly climbed up the last stretch of path that had been worn out by so many generations of the Hart family. The moment the panorama peeked into view, her heart felt light and her spirits lifted even higher. "I just love this place."

"I know."

Leaning back against him, his arms looped around her, they stood silently soaking in the views that had graced this mountain for hundreds of years.

"Come on." He eased away, the loss of touch almost painful, and tugged at her hand. "Let's sit."

From now till the next millennium, she could sit on the old family bench that had been carved by the first Hart to settle this land. Having a man like David at her side to appreciate the view and the bench made it all the sweeter.

"Zinnia." Seated beside her, David shifted to face her. "I've been thinking about us a lot lately."

She nodded. So had she.

"But this morning, your cousin opened my eyes."

To cake?

"I've tasted a lot of cake in my life too. Heather's right. When you find the right one, you know it. I know it." He slid off the bench, dropped to one knee in front of her and Zinnia felt all the air in her lungs whoosh out. "I know this is a little sudden, probably unexpected, but I don't want to taste any more cake. I know you're the one for me, and if you feel even a little bit the same way, I would love for you to please consider marrying me."

As if she'd eaten a spoonful of peanut butter, her tongue stuck to the roof of her mouth and it took all her energy to form even the simplest word. "Yes!"

His gaze searched her face. Still kneeling, he swallowed hard. "Yes, you feel a little bit the same way, or yes, you'll marry me?"

Not wanting any further confusion, she threw her arms around him, almost toppling him over and kissing his cheek, she muttered, *yes*. Kissing his nose, *yes*, his eyes, *yes*, his lips long and hard. Then she pulled back, her arms still in a strangle hold around his neck. "Yes, I'll marry you. I love you!"

Slipping one hand into his pocket, he pulled something out and maneuvering it between his fingers, slid a cigar band onto her left hand ring finger. "Until you can pick out a ring you like," he squeezed the band tightly, "this placeholder makes it official. I love you, Zinnia Colby soon to be Ingram."

Staring down at her left hand, she bit back a laugh. "I love it."

"It was the General's idea."

"My grandfather, the General?"

"The one and only." He nodded. "I thought it only right I, well, ask permission for your hand since I didn't want to wait to search out your father."

"I gather he said yes."

"And handed me the cigar. When I told him I don't smoke, he rolled his eyes at me and told me to use the band."

"No lecture, no fuss?"

He shook his head.

"That's a surprise. He never misses a chance to give the ranks a life lesson."

"I thought so too."

"Does your grandfather know?"

David nodded. "While you and Lucy were squeezing lemons, I gave him a quick call from the hall before I knocked on the General's door."

"You did?" She couldn't quite put her finger on it, but there was a connection there, she was sure.

"Is there a problem? I know it's old fashioned and rather unconventional, but—"

She put her fingertips on his lips. "It's perfect. On this mountain, this bench, this old-fashioned world, you're perfect."

"Did I mention I love you?"

Her cheeks almost hurt from smiling so hard. "Feel free to say it again as often as you like."

"Deal, future Mrs. Ingram. Deal."

CHAPTER SEVENTEEN ~ EPILOGUE

"**I** can't believe this day is finally here."

"I can't believe I'm not wearing a yellow dress." Poppy glanced down at the pale aqua toned gown with a sheath skirt and thanked heaven she didn't look like a sunflower.

"Yellow?" Jake's friend and her groomsman partner, Brent, seemed confused.

"Originally she'd picked out these rather, shall we say, hideous dresses."

Callie waved an arm at her sister. "Coming from the only one in the family who loves to wear skirts, calling those dresses hideous really means something."

"Ooh, I forgot how much I liked the crab puffs at the tasting." Zinnia licked the tips of her fingers. "Don't tell Grams you saw that."

Poppy dragged her fingers across her mouth. "My lips are sealed."

"Let me take care of it." David came up beside his fiancée, and holding her hand, licked the already clean fingertips. Poppy couldn't decide if that was sweet or ridiculous, until he leaned over and kissed the tip of her nose and mouthed, *I love you Mrs. Ingram.* Definitely sweet. Those two were crazy perfect for each other.

Post ceremony photographs taken, the bridal party got what was probably going to be their only chance to sample the appetizers currently being served to the guests. Friends and family were mulling about the main hall, enjoying the cocktail hour and awaiting the official start of the reception. Poppy and the others were trying very hard to not be nervous about parading across the dance floor. They'd all practiced their shtick for a few minutes during the rehearsal yesterday. It wasn't really a big deal, most guests only wanted to see the bride and groom's entrance.

Giggling from the corner of the room caught her attention and she spotted David twirling Zinnia in place. Spending time with them the last few days as the wedding drew near, she was intrigued by how often the two of them had their heads together just smiling or laughing. For one of the more serious of her cousins, Zinnia was certainly full of smiles these days.

"It's time." The wedding coordinator clapped her hands and stood guard at the door, ushering everyone out of the room.

At the bottom of the steps, her assistant kept the group corralled, awaiting the signal. Counting heads like a school bus driver, she double checked the entire bridal party was present and ready to be introduced. The woman must've started counting from front to back of the line at least two or three times. Clearly sixteen was above her skill set.

Poppy had an overwhelming urge to order her sisters and cousins to do a sound off. Somewhat appropriate for the grandchildren of a Marine Corps general, but she decided not to make the woman any more nervous than she already was. "We're all here."

The music began and her sister Callie and Zane were the first to hurry up the stairs, do a twirl and flair as their names were announced and then dashed away from the spotlight to the bridal party tables. Next was Zinnia and David. A quick kiss for luck and holding hands, they were off and up the stairs. Like Callie before them, they did a fancy twirl but closed with an impressive dip. For two seconds Poppy almost thought Zinnia's head would hit the floor, but up she came laughing, another quick peck on the lips and they too darted away from the spotlight. Three more cousins up and done and it was Poppy's turn. Brent grabbed her hand, whispered to her to relax, and before she knew it she'd been up and down and praise God hadn't tripped over Brent or her dress.

By the time her heart stopped pounding the DJ announced the new Mr. and Mrs. Harper, and up came Heather and Jake. The song changed and the two began waltzing around the dance floor. A wall of glass windows revealed a view of the sparkling moonlit lake for all to see and, in the distance, the Point. Up the hill behind the favorite family gathering place, lit like a guiding light, Hart House stood proud in all its heartwarming glory. The perfect backdrop to the perfect couple after a perfect wedding. A twirl, a spin, and Heather and Jake fell easily back into the traditional steps. The crowd remained riveted on the pair. Not even the breathtaking views could steal their attention. Poppy needed a chair. The excitement had gotten the best of her.

"Would you like some water?" Brent asked. "You look a bit pale."

"Oh. Thank you." Her gaze traced his back as he went off to the bar. Halfway between the table and the bar, tucked back in the shadows, Zinnia and David stood watching the newly married couple. But unlike the other onlookers, Zinnia was leaning back in the fold of David's arms, the two of them swaying side to side to the gentle rhythm of Al Green's "Let's Stay Together," with an occasional whisper in the other's ear, followed by a smile or soft laugh.

"They look pretty good together, don't they?" Brent handed her the glass of water.

"They do."

"He seems like a nice guy."

"Yeah. He does."

The dance came to an end and that was their cue. Not wanting to delay the start of the dancing, the bridesmaids and groomsmen were ready to rush to the floor for the official opening dance. The Macarena. Not one of Poppy's favorites, it held sentimental value to Heather and her dad so the Macarena she would do.

Within minutes, almost all the guests were hip slapping and jump spinning with utter glee. Apparently the song held a lot of memories for a lot of people. Once again, her gaze settled on her cousin. Something about Zinnia and David was compelling to watch. All her cousins had made great matches, but she would venture of all the engaged couples, these two would be the next to tie the knot.

"It's a good party." Her grandfather came to stand beside her.

"With Aunt Rebecca, in charge I would expect nothing less."

The General chuckled. "Agreed. Those two seem to have found their rhythm quickly."

Poppy followed his chin and was willing to bet money that he was pointing to Zinnia and David as well. "That's what I thought."

Her gaze still centered on her newly engaged cousin, her grandfather leaned in closer. "Your turn is coming."

On a long sigh, she looked up at him. There couldn't possibly be any more good men left within a thousand miles. "I don't know about that."

Smiling, the General straightened to his full height, put his hands behind his back at parade rest and nodded. "I do."

From Lily's Recipe Box

AUNT TRISH'S SWEET CORNBREAD

What you'll need:

1 cup cornmeal
1 cup flour
1 tbsp baking powder
1 tbsp sugar
1/4 tsp salt
1 cup milk
¼ cup oil
2 large eggs
2 tbsp honey (last ingredient to add)

Instructions:

Combine milk, oil, and eggs together, then add dry ingredients.
After mixing all the ingredients, drizzle 2 tbsps of honey on top and stir lightly into mix.
Pour into a greased 9" round cast iron skillet or pan (Lily recommends an iron skillet for the nice crunch on the bottom)
Place into a 375 preheated oven for about 30 minutes.

Excerpt from POPPY

PROLOGUE

"I don't see any way around this. Dylan isn't easy."

"I beg your pardon?" General Richard Powell, U.S. Marine Corps Retired, spoke up via Zoom from the tablet perched on the credenza. "What's wrong with my grandson?"

"Face it. He's not in local real estate, he doesn't fish, he's not in charge of an annual picnic, and he doesn't need a place to stow away to write the great American novel. We've been at this for hours. There's simply no way to bring these two together."

"It doesn't help any that his work isn't exactly portable." Cole's granddad, Captain Donald McIntyre USN Retired, shrugged.

"We just need to think harder." Harold knew his Poppy and Dick's grandson Dylan would be perfect for each other. They just needed to come up with a casual way to *accidentally* get them in the same place at the same time.

"Why is this match so difficult? We're eight for eight and it never took this long to come up with an idea." Jake's grandfather, Commander Eugene Harper USN Retired, heaved a deep sigh.

Flipping his palm face up, Don made a who-the-hell-knows gesture. "Maybe it's the church."

"What does the church have to do with anything?" Gene lifted his gaze from the cards in his hand.

"Something about playing cards in the pastor's counseling office doesn't feel right."

"Too risky getting together at Hart House and having someone overhear or put eight and eight together. Besides, it's not like we're playing poker or betting."

Don shrugged. "You're right. We're not plotting to rob the Pope or anything nefarious. Just giving two people well suited to each other a little nudge toward happily ever after. That's sort of the Lord's work."

"It is a nice church." Frank's gaze danced around them at the dark wood paneling, the intricately carved trim work surrounding the built-in bookcases, and the exquisite murals on the ceiling and walls reminiscent of the great churches of Europe. "What is it, a hundred years old?"

"Almost two hundred." The old fieldstone-based building with cedar shingles and a wooden steeple tower that could be seen almost to the next county had been the heart of Lawford Mountain for generations. "The stained glass windows are newer. About a hundred and twenty years or so. When we leave I'll take you into the sanctuary. The handcrafted features and hand-painted murals will leave you in awe. The sad thing is that anything this old needs lots of reworking. The plumbing is constantly leaking and the tree roots are in constant battle with the sewer lines. When I offered the pastor a little donation to use the church on his day off for my men's club meeting, he was quick to accept."

"I'll chip in some," one of the voices added, followed by another and another.

Frank nodded. "I'm in too. Now, back to the final match. You said Poppy works here long hours?"

"Some days, yes. Depends on what the church board is up to and how much backup the pastor needs." Harold reached into his pocket and handed out four Cuban cigars, one for each of his buddies and one for himself. "Maybe this will help inspire us. Since there's no bourbon here, next best thing is a good smoke."

"Where did you get these?"

Harold bit back a smile. "I still have a few connections."

"You're not supposed to be smoking those," Dick's voice boomed from the nearby tablet.

"It's been over a year since this damn rollercoaster ride started. I'm doing great. Fit as a fiddle. Monthly treatments are over. I've been promoted to every six months for follow up." Harold wouldn't admit—even to his lifelong buddies—that he'd been scared to death when diagnosed, and had been lucky as hell that all he'd needed to fight this miserable disease was outpatient surgery and monthly immunotherapy.

"That does sound good." Don focused on his playing cards. "I'll bid two."

"It is. At this point one cigar won't hurt. The best war games were planned with a stiff drink whenever possible, but always with a cigar." As challenging as the diagnosis over a year ago had been, at least it had spurred him on when it came to his granddaughters. He'd waited long enough for them to make their own matches. It was time.

"Hal's right. All it took was a few turns of the wrench and when that faucet fell off, my Jake was practically on his way down the aisle." Gene set his cigar in the make-shift ashtray. "Pass."

"And despite the tragedy of Adele, we managed to get Eric and the kids to Hart Land."

"In the knick of time too." Retired Marine Corps Colonel Francis—Frank—Peterson peered over the cards in his hands.

"Why didn't Gil fly in?" Don asked about Iris' grandfather-in-law, Captain Gilbert Johnson USN Retired.

"Fishing with his son." Frank smiled at his cards. "Four."

"You know I can't pass up a four bid." Harold reached for the kitty of cards in the middle of the table.

"I know." Frank grinned. "Some things haven't changed one iota since Annapolis. I almost said five."

Ignoring Dick's contented smirk, Harold slid the four new cards into his hand. He and his academy cohorts had three more days together before Gene and Frank had to fly home. Something would come to mind. It had to. Making multiple grandfathers visiting at the same time look like a coincidence hadn't been easy. Of course, there was always Fate. She did a pretty good job at improvisation. Lily hitting Cole with her car had been sheer genius on her part. Not that he wished Dylan to be hit by a car, but Harold was confident between the four of them here in this room and the rest of their matchmaking troops available when needed, thanks to the modern cyber world, a plan would be hatched sooner or later.

Don took a puff of his cigar and moved the ashtray out of the way and onto the small cabinet under the nearby window. "We could wait for winter and pray for an avalanche."

"An avalanche?" Harold stopped sorting his cards.

"Yeah, you know, like that movie where the men and women were all snowbound in a small cabin for the winter. Spent most of the time dancing."

"*Seven Brides for Seven Brothers*?" Frank frowned.

"Maybe." Don shrugged.

"We're not waiting till winter, and we're not burying anyone under an avalanche of snow." Harold set four cards aside. Crazy stunts like that were his housekeeper Lucy's type of shenanigans, and even *she* wouldn't go that far. "Clubs are trump."

Frank sniffed at the air. "How old is the wiring in this place?"

"Old enough. Why?" A familiar and unpleasant smell tickled at Harold's nose.

The other card players paused and sniffed.

"Something's burning." Don pushed to his feet and his eyes grew wide as he reached for the cigar that was no longer on the cabinet.

Arm straight out, Gene pointing at the large window behind them just as a burst of flames exploded from the trash can. "Where's the fire extinguisher?"

"In the hall!" someone shouted.

The flames licked at the edge of the old velvet drapes. Don kicked the wastebasket away as the other men lurched toward the window, too late to prevent the drapes from going up in flames.

"Oh, hell." Now Frank was stomping on the burning papers scattered across the throw rug atop two hundred year old pine floors.

Gene hurried back into the small room. "Oh, sh—"

Beating at the fiery rug with the shirts off their backs and the flames spreading to piles of papers despite their efforts, and the extinguisher, Harold stopped and whipped out his phone. No sense going through dispatch, Cole was on speed dial. "The church is on fire."

By the time the sound of sirens had the men rushing outdoors, the pastor had come from his house across the street and turned on the garden hose. Don commandeered the neighbor's hose and watered down the cedar shingles. Harold gave a silent prayer of thanks that the place wasn't totally engulfed in tongues of fire. The Lord had one heck of a way of reminding him smoking cigars was not good for his health. Or anyone else's. Especially a two hundred year old wooden building. Fiona was going to kill him.

"I don't know how the ashtray tipped over." His face painted with guilt, Don stood at his side.

"That was my fault." Gene sighed. "I bumped the cabinet with my foot. Probably knocked it over."

"I was sitting right there." Lips pressed tightly together, Don shook his head. "I should have heard the thing fall into the basket. Should have moved the basket."

"It could have been me," Harold said. "My ashtray was on the other end. Maybe I nudged it. What matters is we did our best to contain it."

The fire trucks pulled up, and like ants escaping a knocked over hill, scurrying to protect their larvae, firemen ran in every direction. Hoses spewed water at the historical building. The sound of smashed glass filled the air and Harold bit down hard on his back teeth, praying the noise wasn't one of the ancient stained glass windows or the treasured artwork.

"That couldn't be good."

"Or could it?" Frank tipped his head and turned to his friends, smiling.

For a moment Harold thought senility had taken over Frank's thoughts. Then he got it. A slow grin tugged at his cheeks. "I'll be. Fate—and the firemen—did it again."

CHAPTER ONE

"**I** feel like a soggy rat after a flash flood." Poppy stood at her desk. The Lawford Mountain Community Church had survived almost 200 years of winter, rain, drought, feast and famine. She wasn't so sure it was going to survive one cigar.

"It's not that bad." Pastor Robert Sullivan, her boss for the most part and known to all as Bob, smiled at her as if all the pieces of paper on or in her desk hadn't inflated like a sponge to three times its size.

Well, not in width and length, but the few sheets that had dried since the firemen turned off the torrent of water were stacked much higher, and many no longer fit in folders.

"The water restoration people should be here any minute," the pastor reminded her. They'd been called as soon as the firemen left the scene and informed him and church board that the building hadn't sustained enough structural damage to preclude any efforts at rescue.

Her gaze traveled from one corner of the room to the other and out the doorway. Even in the brief amount of time it had taken the local fire department to put out the rapidly spreading fire, it had been more than enough time to soak the few rugs the church offices had. Scurrying to salvage as much as possible, she'd sloshed through the water along with half the town. People had come with their own push brooms and floor mops in an effort to drain the pooling water away from the old pine floors. The sorry scene almost made her want to cry. The church was already struggling to keep up with this beautiful, but old, edifice. They really didn't need fire and flood on top of everyday wear and tear.

Hands on her hips, Lucy nodded. "I agree with the pastor. We did a darned good job."

"You'll earn extra rewards in heaven for this." Grams stood on tippy toe and kissed Zinnia's fiancé, David's, cheek. "If we had to wait for the flood restoration people to get here before removing all this water, these floors would've been ruined."

"And the walls," Jake, the most recent grandson-in-law added to the clan, said. "Sheetrock soaks up water faster than a thirsty man fresh out of the desert."

The turnout from town to help had been heartwarming. Jake had brought over every floor squeegee and wet vacuum he had in stock at the hardware store. Mabel had contributed a nonstop supply of hot coffee and tea. Poppy's sister Lily had kept all the volunteers energized with both sugary and protein-heavy treats from the Pastry Stop. Katie kept everyone hydrated with bottles of water and sports drinks.

At one point, with so many bodies bumping into each other trying to sweep the water out the door, vacuum up the water, or carry out whatever treasured pieces of furniture and artwork weren't bolted down, the pastor finally had to send some people home and ask them to please just pray. Poppy wanted to also suggest they give a little extra in next week's collection box, but decided if ever there was a time to keep her mouth closed, this would be one of them. People had given so much already.

Glancing out the window, the front yard of the church looked like a sorry attempt at a tag sale. The merry widows and most of her cousins were toweling down the wooden furniture they'd successfully removed before it soaked up anymore of the water. Some neighbors held blow dryers plugged into orange extension cords and aimed at the furniture to help with the deep-down drying. Metal cabinets and wastebaskets were scattered about. At least odds were in their favor that the sun would continue to shine until it was safe to move all the belongings back inside.

"You look awfully pensive." Her grandmother slipped an arm around her waist. "It will be fine. You'll see."

"I know." Somewhere deep in her heart Poppy knew everything would work out, but the images in the back of her mind stuttered her heart every step of the way. Obviously the curtains were gone and would have to be replaced along with the scorched walls, and probably smoke stained ceiling. But it was the gorgeous artwork that normally hung in the counselling room that left her so doubtful. How would they undo the smoke and water damage? With all their other woes, she wasn't sure the church carried enough insurance for the cost of such a major undertaking.

"You're still frowning." Grams wiped at her forehead with her thumb. "Have I ever lied to you?"

That brought a smile to Poppy's face. "No, ma'am."

"There you go." Grams retreated a step, her linked fingers lingering slightly until she fully let go. "Now let's see if we can find out how long thoroughly drying this place out is going to take, or if we need to set an office up for you and Pastor Bob at Hart House."

Wiggling her toes within her damp shoes, Poppy looked down at her soiled and slightly torn skirt. The thing had seen better days. Maybe camping out at Hart House for work would be the silver lining on today's fire. Actually, an angel from heaven appearing out of thin air and putting the place back together the way it was— murals, craftsmanship, and all—would be perfect. After all, she really *did* believe in miracles.

• • • •

"Oh, that does look beautiful." General Richard—Dick—Powell smiled at his grandson. "Your grandmother is going to love this."

"I certainly hope so." Dylan had to agree with his grandfather that the odds were pretty good his grandmother would indeed love the painting. The project was definitely turning out better than he'd expected. It had been years since he'd attempted anything original for his own pleasure. The hope was that this portrait of his sister's children and his grandmother would be the perfect gift for her upcoming birthday.

From the other room he could hear his business line ring and the phone's answering machine pick up. Screening calls was a necessity when he was deep in a project. "This is Pastor Bob Sullivan from Lawford Mountain in New England. We've had a recent... *incident* at our church and would like to get an idea of your fees and availability." The man hesitated a long beat before adding, simply, "Thank you."

His grandfather's gaze darted back and forth to the hall doorway and back to Dylan, almost intentionally averting the phone as if it might reach out and bite him. What was that all about?

The business line rang again.

Having kept his focus on the painting in front of him, he'd barely paid attention to the previous caller. A second call within minutes had his head snapping up.

"This is General Harold Hart. I've been told on good authority that you're the best in the business. You should be hearing soon from Pastor Robert Sullivan. The church will of course be having a bazaar or some other event to raise funds for your services, as well as your travel expenses from Texas." The voice cleared his throat. "I would like to make a major— anonymous—contribution to the fund. Please get in touch with me as soon as possible." The rough voice that sounded every bit a Marine disconnected the call. Though for all Dylan knew, army generals sounded as rough and gruff as Marine Corps generals. Maybe even the air force. But a general *and* a pastor? An interesting combination off the battle field. "Odd."

"What is?" His granddad frowned at the canvass in front of Dylan.

"Not the painting. The two phone calls."

"What's so odd about two phone calls?" On that question the phone rang one more time.

Once again, the voicemail system kicked in. "Hello Mr. Powell, this is Nadine Baker. Your name has been floated around as someone who can be trusted with a two hundred year old building."

Poised for the next stroke, the hand holding the paint brush lowered slowly to the palette of pastel colors. The words *two hundred year old* had caught his attention.

"The town will of course be responsible for your fee, but the

Merry Wid—my women's group—would like to contribute anonymously to the cause."

Today seemed to be the day for charitable hearts.

"If you could kindly return my call to discuss figures before you speak with Pastor Sullivan, that would be very nice. Thank you."

"That's what's odd about *three* phone calls." Now he put the palette down on the nearby table, swirled his brush in the jar, and let his mind turn with curiosity.

"This can't be the first time you've had three phone calls in a day."

"Perhaps not in a day, but certainly back to back and all about a pastor."

"You mean a church." Lowering his chin to peer at his grandson over the brim of his eyeglasses, the retired general's voice dropped a few notches as well. "I know you've done church restorations before."

He had. It was some of his favorite work, depending on the need. The two projects in Italy had been his most favorites. "Yes."

"So what makes these calls so odd?"

"Usually I deal with one person and any anonymous donations are made to the church, not to me."

"Oh, well. I wouldn't know about that." His grandfather took a step back and a deep breath. "Are you interested?"

Keeping quiet, Dylan proceeded to clean his brushes. He'd pick up again tomorrow in better light and with a clear head. "Maybe." Truth was, he was more than interested. How many chances did a man have to work in the United States on two hundred year old artwork? But it was his grandfather's curiosity that had his interest at the moment "So, what aren't you telling me?"

As expected, his grandfather snapped around. Eyes wide with surprise—or guilt—blinked, dropping the military veil of authority to hide whatever was going on in that complex mind of his.

"What makes you ask that?"

"Just a hunch." Something about the way his grandfather looked lost somewhere between awkward and uncomfortable made him think perhaps the old man knew more than he was letting on. Though what the connection could be between his grandfather and an ancient small town church was beyond him. Maybe he'd been watching too many reruns of *Law and Order*, he was developing a cynical mind.

His granddad hesitated, seeming to search for his words. Another oddity in its own right. The former Marine Corps general was never at a loss for words. "There isn't much to tell. Recently a friend mentioned there's been a fire at his local church. A very old building with murals. Stories got kicked around about restoring the Mona Lisa and the Sistine Chapel and somewhere in there your name and the recent job you did for the Atlanta Museum of Art came up."

"The Mona Lisa has never been fully restored. Too risky."

"Yes, that was mentioned. Anyhow, these calls may or may not have something to do with that recent conversation. After all, you are one of the best in the country. Why shouldn't they want you?"

Well, there was nothing nefarious in his grandfather discussing art or bringing up that Dylan was indeed a conservator/restorer of fine art by trade. And his reputation had indeed grown to national recognition in recent years. So why did he have this strange nagging feeling, reminiscent of a small spider loose and crawling up his back?

MEET CHRIS

USA TODAY Bestselling Author of more than a dozen contemporary novels, including the award-winning *Champagne Sisterhood*, Chris Keniston lives in suburban Dallas with her husband, two human children, and two canine children. Though she loves her puppies equally, she admits being especially attached to her German Shepherd rescue. After all, even dogs deserve a happily ever after.

More on Chris and her books can be found at
www.chriskeniston.com

Follow Chris on Facebook at ChrisKenistonAuthor
or on Twitter @ckenistonauthor

Questions? Comments?
I would love to hear from you.
You can reach me at chris@chriskeniston.com

www.ingramcontent.com/pod-product-compliance
Lightning Source LLC
Chambersburg PA
CBHW030935060726
47591CB00005B/1803